AN EPISODE IN THE
LIFE OF A LANDSCAPE
PAINTER

CÉSAR AIRA

AN EPISODE IN THE LIFE OF A LANDSCAPE PAINTER

Preface by ROBERTO BOLAÑO

Translated from the Spanish by CHRIS ANDREWS

A New Directions Paperbook Original

Copyright © 2000 by César Aira
Translation copyright © 2006 by Chris Andrews

Originally published by Beatriz Viterbo Editora, Argentina, as *Un episodio en la vida del pintor Viajero*, in 2000; published by arrangement with the Michael Gaeb Literary Agency, Berlin.

The preface, "The Incredible César Aira" *(El increíble César Aira)* by Roberto Bolaño, was originally published in *Entre paréntesis* in 2004 by Editorial Anagrama; © Heirs of Roberto Bolaño, 2004.

Manufactured in the United States of America
New Directions Books are printed on acid-free paper.
First published as a New Directions Paperbook Original (NDP1035) in 2006
Published simultaneously in Canada by Penguin Books Canada Limited

Library of Congress Cataloging-in-Publication Data
Aira, César, 1949–
[Episodio en la vida del pintor viajero. English]
An episode in the life of a landscape painter / César Aira ; preface by Roberto Bolaño ; translated from the Spanish by Chris Andrews.
p. cm.
ISBN-13: 978-0-8112-1630-2 (alk. paper)
ISBN-10: 0-8112-1630-6 (alk. paper)
I. Andrews, Chris. II. Title.
PQ7798.1.I7E6513 2006
863'.64—dc22

2005035053

15 14 13 12 11

New Directions Books are published for James Laughlin
by New Directions Publishing Corporation
80 Eighth Avenue, New York, New York 10011
ndbooks.com

Preface

The Incredible César Aira
by Roberto Bolaño

If there is one contemporary writer who defies classification, it is César Aira, an Argentinean from a town in the province of Buenos Aires called Coronel Pringles, which must, I suppose, be a real place, although it could well have been imagined by its most eminent son, who has given us superlatively lucid portraits of the Mother (a verbal mystery) and the Father (a geometrical certitude), and whose position in contemporary Hispanic literature is equal in complexity to that of Macedonio Fernández at the beginning of the twentieth century.

Let me start by saying that Aira has written one of the five best stories I can remember. The story, included in Juan Forn's anthology *Buenos Aires*, is entitled "Cecil Taylor." He is also the author of four memorable novels: *How I Became a Nun*, in which he recounts his childhood; *Ema, The Captive*, in which he recounts the opulence of the pampas Indians; *The Literature Conference*, in which he recounts an attempt to clone Carlos Fuentes; and *The Crying*, in which he recounts a sort of epiphany or bout of insomnia.

Naturally those are not the only novels he has written. I am told that Aira writes two books a year, at least, some of which are published by a little Argentinean company named Beatriz Viterbo, after the character in Borges's story "The Aleph." The books of his that I have been able to find were published by Mondadori and Tusquets Argentina. It's frustrating, because once you've started reading Aira, you don't want to stop. His novels seem to put the theories of Gombrowicz into practice, except, and the difference is fundamental, that Gombrowicz was the abbot of a luxurious imaginary monastery, while Aira is a nun or novice among the Discalced Carmelites of the Word. Sometimes he is reminiscent of Roussel (Roussel on his knees in a bath red with blood), but the only living writer to whom he can be compared is Barcelona's Enrique Vila-Matas.

Aira is an eccentric, but he is also one of the three or four best writers working in Spanish today.

AN EPISODE IN THE LIFE OF A LANDSCAPE PAINTER

WESTERN ART can boast few documentary painters of true distinction. Of those whose lives and work we know in detail, the finest was Rugendas, who made two visits to Argentina. The second, in 1847, gave him an opportunity to record the landscapes and physical types of the Río de la Plata—in such abundance that an estimated two hundred paintings remained in the hands of local collectors—and to refute his friend and admirer Humboldt, or rather a simplistic interpretation of Humboldt's theory, according to which the painter's talent should have been exercised solely in the more topographically and botanically exuberant regions of the New World. But the refutation had in fact been foreshadowed ten years earlier, during Rugendas's brief and dramatic first visit, which was cut short by a strange episode that would mark a turning point in his life.

Johann Moritz Rugendas was born in the imperial city of Augsburg on the 29th of March 1802. His father, grandfather and great-grandfather were all well-known genre painters; one of his ancestors, Georg Philip Rugendas, was famous for his battle scenes. The Rugendas family (although Flemish in origin) had emigrated from Catalonia in 1608 and settled in Augsburg, hoping to find a social environment more hospitable to its Protestant faith. The first German Rugendas was a master clockmaker; all the rest were painters. Johann Moritz confirmed his vocation at the age of four. A gifted draftsman, he was an outstanding student at the studio of Albrecht Adam and then at the Munich Art Academy. When he was nineteen, an opportunity arose to join the expedition to America led by Baron Langsdorff and financed by the Czar of Russia. His mission was one that, a hundred years later, would have fallen to a photographer: to keep a graphic record of all the discoveries they would make and the landscapes through which they would pass.

At this point, to get a clearer idea of the work upon which the young artist was embarking, it is necessary to go back in time. It was Johan Moritz's great-grandfather, Georg Philip Rugendas (1666–1742) who founded the dynasty of painters. And he did so as a result of losing his right hand as a young man. The mutilation rendered him unfit for the family trade of clockmaking, in which he had been trained since childhood. He had to learn to use his left hand, and to manipulate pencil and brush. He specialized in the depiction of battles, with excellent results, due to the preternatural precision of his draftsmanship, which was due in turn to his training as a clockmaker and the use of his left hand, which, not being his spontaneous choice, obliged him to work with methodical deliberation. An exquisite contrast between the petrified intricacy of the form and the violent turmoil of the subject matter made him unique. His protector and principal patron was Charles XII of Sweden, the warrior king, whose battles he painted, following the armies from the hyperborean snows to sun-scorched Turkey. In later years he became a prosperous printer and publisher of engravings—a natural extension of his skills in military documentation. His three sons, Georg Philip, Johan and Jeremy, inherited both the business and the skills. Christian (1775–1826), the son of Georg Philip junior, was the father of our Rugendas, who brought the cycle to a close by painting the battles of another warrior king, Napoleon.

Napoleon's fall ushered in a "century of peace" in Europe, so inevitably the branch of the profession in which the family had specialized went into decline. Young Johan Moritz, an adolescent at the time of Waterloo, was obliged to execute a swift change of direction. Initially apprenticed to Adam, a battle painter, he began taking classes in nature painting at the Munich Academy. The "nature" favored by buyers of paintings and prints was exotic and remote, so he would have to follow his artistic calling abroad, and the direction his travels would take was soon determined by the opportunity to participate in the voyage mentioned above. On the threshold of his twentieth year, the world that opened before him was roughly mapped out yet still unexplored, much as it was, at around the same time, for the young Charles Darwin. The German painter's Fitzroy was Baron Georg Heinrich von Langsdorff, who, during the crossing of the Atlantic turned out to be so "obdurate and harebrained" that when the boat arrived in Brazil, Rugendas parted company with the expedition, and was replaced by another talented documentary painter, Taunay. By this decision he spared himself a good deal of grief, for the voyage was ill-starred: Taunay drowned in the Guaporé River and in the middle of the jungle Langsdorff lost what few wits he had. Rugendas, meanwhile, after four years of travel and work in the provinces of Rio de Janeiro, Minas Gerais, Mato Grosso, Espiritu Santo and Bahia, returned to Europe and published an exquisite illustrated book entitled *A Picturesque Voyage through Brazil* (the text was written by Victor Aimé Huber using the painter's notes), which made him famous and put him in touch with the eminent naturalist Alexander von Humboldt, with whom he was to collaborate on a number of publications.

Rugendas's second and final voyage to America lasted seventeen years, from 1831 to 1847. His industrious journeying took him to Mexico, Chile, Peru, Brazil again and Argentina, and resulted in hundreds, indeed thousands of paintings. (An incomplete catalogue, including oil paintings, watercolors and drawings, numbers 3353 works.) Although the Mexican phase is the best represented, and tropical jungles and mountain scenes constitute his most characteristic subject matter, the secret aim of this long voyage, which consumed his youth, was Argentina: the mysterious emptiness to be found on the endless plains at a point equidistant from the horizons. Only there, he thought, would he be able to discover the other side of his art ... This dangerous illusion pursued him throughout his life. Twice he crossed the threshold: in 1837, he came over the Andes from Chile, and in 1847, he approached from the east, via the Río de la Plata. The second expedition was the more productive, but did not take him beyond the environs of Buenos Aires; on his first journey, however, he ventured towards the dreamed-of center and in fact reached it momentarily, although, as we shall see, the price he had to pay was exorbitant.

Rugendas was a genre painter. His genre was the physiognomy of nature, based on a procedure invented by Humboldt. The great naturalist was the father of a discipline that virtually died with him: *Erdtheorie* or *La Physique du monde*, a kind of artistic geography, an aesthetic understanding of the world, a science of landscape. Alexander von Humboldt (1769–1859) was an all-embracing scholar, perhaps the last of his kind: his aim was to apprehend the world in its totality; and the way to do this, he believed, in conformity with a long tradition, was through vision. Yet his approach was new in that, rather than isolating images and treating them as "emblems" of knowledge, his aim was to accumulate and coordinate them within a broad framework, for which landscape provided the model. The artistic geographer had to capture the "physiognomy" of the landscape (Humboldt had borrowed this concept from Lavater) by picking out its characteristic "physiognomic" traits, which his scholarly studies in natural science would enable him to recognize. The precise arrangement of physiognomic elements in the picture would speak volumes to the observer's sensibility, conveying information not in the form of isolated features but features systematically interrelated so as to be intuitively grasped: climate, history, customs, economy, race, fauna, flora, rainfall, prevailing winds ... The key to it all was "natural growth," which is why the vegetable element occupied the foreground, and why, in search of physiognomic landscapes, Humboldt went to the tropics, which were incomparably superior to Europe in terms of plant variety and rates of growth. He lived for many years in tropical regions of Asia and America, and encouraged the artists who had adopted his approach to do likewise. Thus he established a circuit, stimulating curiosity in Europe about regions that were still little known and creating a market for the works of the traveling painters.

Humboldt had the highest admiration for the young Rugendas, whom he dubbed the "founding father of the art of pictorial presentation of the physiognomy of nature," a description that could well have applied to himself. He played an advisory role in the painter's second great voyage, and the only point on which they disagreed was the decision to include Argentina in the itinerary. Humboldt did not want his disciple to waste his efforts south of the tropical zone, and in his letters he was generous with recommendations such as the following: "Do not squander your talent, which is suited above all to the depiction of that which is truly exceptional in landscape, such as snowy mountain peaks, bamboo, tropical jungle flora, groups composed of a single plant species at different ages; *filiceae*, *Lataniae*, feathery-fronded palms, bamboo, cylindrical cactuses, red-flowered mimosas, the inga tree with its long branches and broad leaves, shrub-sized malvaceous plants with digitate leaves, particularly the Mexican hand plant (*Cheirantodendron*) in Toluca; the famous ahuehuete of Atlisco (the thousand-year-old *Cupressus disticha*) in the environs of Mexico City; the species of orchids that flower beautifully on the rounded, moss-covered protuberances of tree trunks, surrounded in turn by mossy bulbs of *Dendrobium*; the forms of fallen mahogany branches covered with orchids, *Banisteriae* and climbing plants; gramineous species from the bamboo family reaching heights of twenty to thirty feet, Bignoniaceae and the varieties of *foliis distichis*; studies of *Pothos* and *Dracontium*; a trunk of *Crescentia cujete* laden with calabashes; a flowering *Teobroma cacao* with flowers springing up from the roots; the external roots of *Cupressus disticha*, up to four feet tall, shaped like stakes or planks; studies of a rock covered with fucus; blue water lilies in water; *Guastavia* (pirigara) and flowering lecitis; a tropical jungle viewed from a vantage point high on a mountain, showing only the broad crowns of flowering trees, from which the bare trunks of the palms rise like a colonnade, another jungle on top of the jungle; the differing material physiognomies of pisang and heliconium ..."

The excess of primary forms required to characterize a landscape could only be found in the tropics. In so far as vegetation was concerned, Humboldt had reduced these forms to nineteen: nineteen physiognomic types that had nothing to do with Linnean classification, which is based on the abstraction and isolation of minimal differences. The Humboldtian naturalist was not a botanist but a landscape artist sensitive to the processes of growth operative in all forms of life. This system provided the basis for the "genre" of painting in which Rugendas specialized.

After a brief stay in Haiti, Rugendas spent three years in Mexico, from 1831 to 1834. Then he went to Chile, where he was to live for eight years, with the exception of his truncated voyage to Argentina, which lasted roughly five months. The original aim had been to travel right across the country to Buenos Aires, and from there to head north to Tucumán, Bolivia and so on. But it was not to be.

He set out at the end of December 1837 from San Felipe de Aconcagua (Chile), accompanied by the German painter Robert Krause, with a small team of horses and mules and two Chilean guides. The plan was to take advantage of the fine summer weather to cross the picturesque passes of the Cordillera at a leisurely pace, stopping to take notes and paint whenever an interesting subject presented itself. And that was what they did.

In a few days—not counting the many spent painting—they were well into the Cordillera. When it rained they could at least make headway, with their papers carefully rolled up in waxed cloth. It was not really rain so much as a benign drizzle, enveloping the landscape in gentle tides of humidity all afternoon. The clouds came down so low they almost landed, but the slightest breeze would whisk them away ... and produce others from bewildering corridors which seemed to give the sky access to the center of the earth. In the midst of these magical alternations, the artists were briefly granted dreamlike visions, each more sweeping than the last. Although their journey traced a zigzag on the map, they were heading straight as an arrow towards openness. Each day was larger and more distant. As the mountains took on weight, the air became lighter and more changeable in its meteoric content, a sheer optics of superposed heights and depths.

They kept barometric records; they estimated wind speed with a sock of light cloth and used two glass capillary tubes containing liquid graphite as an altimeter. The pink-tinted mercury of their thermometer, suspended with bells from a tall pole, preceded them like Diogenes' daylight lamp. The regular hoofbeats of the horses and mules made a distant-seeming sound; though barely audible, it too was a part of the universal pattern of echoes.

Suddenly, at midnight, explosions, rockets, flares, resonating on and on among the immensities of rock and bringing quick splashes of vivid color to those vast austerities: it was the start of 1838, and the two Germans had brought a provision of fireworks for their own private celebration. They opened a bottle of French wine and drank to the new year with the guides. After which they lay down to sleep under the starry sky, waiting for the moon, which emerged in due course from behind the silhouette of a phosphorescent peak, putting a stop to their drowsy listing of resolutions and launching them into true sleep.

Rugendas and Krause got on well and had plenty to talk about, although both were rather quiet. They had traveled together in Chile a number of times, always in perfect harmony. The only thing that secretly bothered Rugendas was the irremediable mediocrity of Krause's painting, which he was not able to praise in all sincerity, as he would have liked. He tried telling himself that genre painting did not require talent, since it was all a matter of following the procedure, but it was no use: the pictures were worthless. He could, however, appreciate his friend's technical accomplishment and above all his good nature. Krause was very young and still had time to choose another path in life. Meanwhile he could enjoy these excursions; they would certainly do him no harm. Krause, for his part, was in awe of Rugendas, and the pleasure they took in each other's company was due in no small measure to the disciple's devotion. The difference in age and talent was not obvious, because Rugendas, at thirty-five, was timid, effeminate and gawky as an adolescent, while Krause's aplomb, aristocratic manners and considerate nature narrowed the gap.

On the fifteenth day they crossed the watershed and began the descent, advancing more rapidly. There was a risk of the mountains becoming a habit, as they obviously were for the guides, who charged by the day. The Germans would be protected against this danger by the exercise of their art, but only in the long term; in the short term, as they acquainted themselves with the surroundings and their representation, the effect was reversed. Riding on slowly or stopping to rest, they passed the time discussing questions of a technical nature. Each novel sight set their tongues in motion as they sought to account for the difference. It should be remembered that the bulk of the work they were doing was preliminary: sketches, notes, jottings. In their papers, drawing and writing were blended; the exploitation of these data in paintings and engravings was reserved for a later stage. Engravings were the key to circulation, and their potentially infinite reproduction had to be considered in detail. The cycle was completed by surrounding the engravings with a text and inserting them into a book.

Krause was not alone in his appreciation of Rugendas's work. It was obvious how well he painted, primarily because of the simplicity he had attained. Everything in his pictures was bathed in simplicity, which gave them a pearly sheen, filled them with the light of a spring day. They were eminently comprehensible, in conformity with the physiognomic principles. And comprehension led to reproduction; not only had his one published book been a commercial success throughout Europe, the engravings illustrating his *Picturesque Voyage through Brazil* had been printed on wallpaper and even used to decorate Sèvres china.

Krause would often refer, half jokingly, to this extraordinary triumph, and in the solitude of the Cordillera, with no one else there to see, Rugendas would smile and accept the compliment, which was accompanied but not undercut by gentle, affectionate mockery. This was the spirit in which he considered the suggestion that a drawing of Aconcagua be used to decorate a coffee cup: the greatest and smallest of things conjoined by the daily labor of a skilled pencil.

Yet it was not so simple to capture the form of Aconcagua, or any given mountain, in a drawing. If the mountain is imagined as a kind of cone endowed with artistic irregularities, it will be rendered unrecognizable by the slightest shift in perspective, because its profile will change completely.

In the course of the crossing they were constantly making thematic discoveries. Themes were important in genre painting. The two artists documented the landscape artistically and geographically, each in accordance with his capacities. And while they could comprehend the vertical, that is the temporal or geological, dimension unaided, since they knew how to recognize schist and slate, carboniferous dendrites and columnar basalts, plants, mosses and mushrooms, when it came to the horizontal or topographical dimension they had to rely on the Chilean guides, who turned out to be an inexhaustible source of names. "Aconcagua" was only one of many.

The landscape's structuring grid of horizontal and vertical lines was overlaid by man-made traces, which were gridlike in turn. The guides responded to reality without preconceptions. The varying weather and the whims of their German clients, whom they regarded with a combination of respect and disdain so reasonable it could hardly offend, made the changeless world they knew by heart resonate with mystery. The Germans, after all, represented the meeting of science and art on equal terms, as well as the convergence, but not the confusion, of two quite distinct degrees of talent.

Travel and painting were entwined like fibers in a rope. One by one, the dangers and difficulties of a route that was tortuous and terrifying at the best of times were transformed and left behind. And it was truly terrifying: it was hard to believe that this was a route used virtually throughout the year by travelers, mule drivers and merchants. Anyone in their right mind would have regarded it as a means of suicide. Near the watershed, at an altitude of two thousand meters, amid peaks disappearing into the clouds, rather than a way of getting from point A to point B, the path seemed to have become quite simply a way of departing from all points at once. Jagged lines, impossible angles, trees growing downwards from ceilings of rock, sheer slopes plunging into mantles of snow under a scorching sun. And shafts of rain thrust into little yellow clouds, agates enveloped in moss, pink hawthorn. The puma, the hare and the snake made up a mountain aristocracy. The horses panted, began to stumble, and it was time to stop for a rest; the mules were perpetually grumpy.

Peaks of mica kept watch over their long marches. How could these panoramas be rendered credible? There were too many sides; the cube had extra faces. The company of volcanos gave the sky interiors. Dawn and dusk were vast optical explosions, drawn out by the silence. Slingshots and gunshots of sunlight rebounded into every recess. Grey expanses hung out to dry forever in colossal silence; airshafts voluminous as oceans. One morning Krause said that he had had nightmares, so their conversations that day and the next turned on moral mechanics and methods of regaining composure. They wondered if one day cities would be built in those mountains. How might that be? Perhaps if there were wars, when they ended, leaving the stone fortresses empty, with their terraced fields, their border posts and mining villages, a hardworking frontier community composed of Chileans and Argentineans could settle there, converting the buildings and the infrastructure. That was Rugendas's idea, probably influenced by the military painting of his ancestors. Krause, on the other hand, in spite of his worldly outlook, was in favor of mystical colonization. A chain of affiliated monasteries perched in the most remote attics of stone could spread new strains of Buddhism deep into the inaccessible realms, and the braying of the long horns would awaken giants and dwarves of Andean industry. We should draw it, they said. But who would believe it?

Rain, sun, two whole days of impenetrable fog, night winds whistling, winds far and near, nights of blue crystal, crystals of ozone. The graph of temperature against the hours of the day was sinuous, but not unpredictable. Nor, in fact, were their visions. The mountains filed so slowly past that the mind amused itself devising constructivist games to replace them.

A series of studies in vertigo occupied them for the best part of a week. They encountered all sorts of mule drivers, and had the most curious conversations with Chileans and Argentineans from Mendoza. They even came across priests, and Europeans, and the guides' uncles and brothers-in-law. But their solitude was soon restored, and the sight of the others receding into the distance was a source of inspiration.

For some years, Rugendas had been experimenting with a new technique: the oil sketch. This was an innovation and has been recognized as such by art history. It was to be exploited systematically by the Impressionists only fifty years later; but the young German artist's only precursors were a handful of English eccentrics, followers of Turner. It was generally thought that the procedure could only produce shoddy work. And in a sense this was true, but ultimately it would lead to a transvaluation of painting. The effect on Rugendas's daily practice was to punctuate the constant flow of preparatory sketches for serial works (engravings or oil paintings) with one-off pieces. Krause did not follow his example; he was content to witness the frenetic production of these pasty little daubs with their clashing acid colors.

Eventually it became clear that they were leaving the mountain landscapes behind. Would they recognize them if they passed that way again? (Not that they had any plans to do so). They had folders full to bursting with souvenirs. "I can still see it in my mind's eye ..." ran the stock phrase. But why the mind's *eye* in particular? They could still feel it on their faces, in their arms, their shoulders, their hair and heels ... throughout their nervous systems. In the glorious evening light of the 20th of January, they wondered at the assembly of silences and air. A drove of mules the size of ants appeared in silhouette on a ridgetop path, moving at a star's pace. The mules were driven by human intelligence and commercial interests, expertise in breeding and bloodlines. Everything was human; the farthest wilderness was steeped with sociability, and the sketches they had made, in so far as they had any value, stood as records of this permeation. The infinite orography of the Cordillera was a laboratory of forms and colors. In the meditative mind of the traveling painter, Argentina opened before them.

But looking back one last time, the grandeur of the Andes reared, wild and enigmatic, excessively wild and enigmatic. For a few days now, descending steadily, they had felt an exhausting heat closing around them. While his soul dreamt on, contemplating that universe of rock from the last lookout, Rugendas's body was bathed in sweat. A wind at high altitude stripped tufts of snow from the peaks and flung them towards the toiling painters, like a devoted servant bringing cones of vanilla ice cream to refresh them.

The landscape revealed by this backward glance revived old doubts and crucial quandaries. Rugendas wondered if he would be able to make his way in the world, if his work, that is, his art, would support him, if he would be able to manage like everyone else ... So far he had, and comfortably, but that was due in part to the energy of youth and the momentum he had acquired through his training at the Academy and elsewhere. Not to mention good luck. He was almost sure that he would not be able to keep it up. What did he have to fall back on? His profession, and practically nothing else. And what if painting failed him? He had no house, no money in the bank, and no talent for business. His father was dead, and for years he had been wandering through foreign lands. This had given him a peculiar perspective on the argument that begins "If other people can do it ..." All the people he came across, in cities or villages, in the jungle or the mountains, had indeed managed to keep going one way or another, but they were in their own environments; they knew what to expect, while he was at the mercy of fickle chance. How could he be sure that the physiognomic representation of nature would not go out of fashion, leaving him helpless and stranded in the midst of a useless, hostile beauty? His youth was almost over in any case, and still he was a stranger to love. He had ensconced himself in a world of fables and fairy tales, which had taught him nothing of practical use, at least he had learnt that the story always goes on, presenting the hero with new and ever more unpredictable choices. Poverty and destitution would simply be another episode. He might end up begging for alms at the door of a South American church. No fear was unreasonable, given his situation.

These reflections occupied pages and pages of a letter to his sister Luise in Augsburg, the first letter he wrote from Mendoza.

For suddenly there they were in Mendoza, a pretty town with treelined streets, the mountains within arm's reach and skies so immutably blue they were boring. It was midsummer; the locals, stunned by the heat, extended their siestas until six in the evening. Luckily the vegetation provided plenty of shade; the foliage filled the air with oxygen, so breathing, when possible, was very restorative.

Armed with letters of introduction from Chilean friends, the travelers stayed at the house of the attentive and hospitable Godoy de Villanueva family. A large house overshadowed by trees, with an orchard and various little gardens.

Three generations inhabited the ancestral home in harmony, and the smaller children rode around on tricycles, which Rugendas duly sketched in his notebooks; he had never seen them before. Those were his first Argentinean sketches, portents of an interest in vehicles that would soon develop unexpectedly.

They spent a delightful month in and around Mendoza and its environs. The locals bent over backwards to welcome the distinguished visitor, who, invariably accompanied by Krause, made the obligatory excursions to the ranges (which were no doubt more interesting for travelers who had come from the other direction), toured the neighboring estates and generally began to soak up the spirit of Argentina, so similar to Chile in that town near the border, and yet, even there, so different. Mendoza was, in effect, the starting point for the long eastward voyage across the pampas to the fabled Buenos Aires, and that gave it a special, unique character. Another notable feature was that all the buildings in the town and the surrounding country looked new; and so they were, since earthquakes ensured that all man-made structures were replaced approximately every five years. Rebuilding stimulated the local economy. Comfortably riding the seismic activity, the ranches supplied the Chilean markets, exploiting the early maturation of the cattle, speeded by the dangers emanating from the underworld. Rugendas would have liked to depict an earthquake, but he was told that it was not a propitious time according to the planetary clock.

Nevertheless, throughout his stay in the region, he kept secretly hoping he might witness a quake, though he was too tactful to say so. In this respect, and in others, his desires were frustrated. Prosaic Mendoza held promises that, for one reason or another, were not fulfilled and which, in the end, prompted their departure.

His other cherished dream was to witness an Indian raid. In that area, they were veritable human typhoons, but, by their nature, refractory to calendars and oracles. It was impossible to predict them: there might be one in an hour's time or none until next year (and it was only January). Rugendas would have paid to paint one. Every morning of that month, he woke up secretly hoping the great day had come. As in the case of the earthquake, it would have been in poor taste to mention this desire. Dissimulation made him hypersensitive to detail. He was not so sure that there was no forewarning. He questioned his hosts at length, supposedly for professional reasons, about the premonitory signs of seismic activity. It seemed they appeared only hours or minutes before the quake: dogs spat, chickens pecked at their own eggs, ants swarmed, plants flowered, etc. But there was no time to do anything. The painter was convinced that an Indian raid would be anticipated by equally abrupt and gratuitous changes in the cultural domain. But he did not have the opportunity to confirm this intuition.

Despite all the delays they allowed themselves, and their habit of letting nature encourage and justify their lingering, it was time to move on. Not only for practical reasons in this case, but also because, over the years, the painter had gradually constructed a personal myth of Argentina, and after a month spent on the threshold, the pull of the interior was stronger than ever.

A few days before their departure, Emilio Godoy organized an excursion to a large cattle ranch ten leagues south of the town. Among the picturesque sites they visited on the trip was a hilltop from which they had a panoramic view of forests and ranges stretching away to the south. According to their host, it was from those wooded corridors that the Indians usually emerged. They came from that direction, and in pursuit of them, on a punitive expedition after a raid, the ranchers of Mendoza had glimpsed astonishing scenes: mountains of ice, lakes, rivers, impenetrable forests. "That's what you should be painting . . ." It was not the first time he had heard this sentence. People had been repeating it for decades, wherever he went. He had learnt to be wary of such advice. How did they know what he should paint? At this point in his career, within reach of the vast emptiness of the pampas, the art most authentically his own was, he felt, drawing him in the opposite direction. In spite of which, Godoy's descriptions set him dreaming. In his imagination, the Indians' realm of ice was more beautiful and mysterious than any picture he was capable of painting.

Meanwhile, what he was capable of painting took a new and rather unexpected, form. In the process of hiring a guide, he came into contact with a supremely fascinating object: the large carts used for journeys across the pampas.

These were contraptions of monstrous size, as if built to give the impression that no natural force could make them budge. The first time he saw one, he gazed at it intently for a long time. Here, at last, in the cart's vast size, he saw the magic of the great plains embodied and the mechanics of flat surfaces finally put to use. He returned to the loading station the next day and the day after, armed with paper and charcoal. Drawing the carts was at once easy and difficult. He watched them setting off on their long voyages. Their caterpillar's pace, which could only be measured in the distance covered per day or per week, provoked a flurry of quick sketches, and perhaps this was not such a paradox in the work of a painter known for his watercolors of hummingbirds, since extremes of movement, slow as well as quick, have a dissolving effect. He set aside the problem of the moving carts—there would be plenty of opportunities to observe them in action during the journey—and concentrated on the unhitched ones.

Because they had only two wheels (that was their peculiarity), they tipped back when unloaded and their shafts pointed up at the sky, at an angle of forty-five degrees. The ends of the shafts seemed to disappear among the clouds; their length can be deduced from the fact that they could be used to hitch ten teams of oxen. The sturdy planks were reinforced to bear immense loads; whole houses, on occasion, complete with furniture and inhabitants. The wheels were like fairground Ferris wheels, made entirely of carob wood, with spokes as thick as roof beams and bronze hubs at the center, laden with pints of grease. To give an idea of the carts' real dimensions, Rugendas had to draw small human figures beside them, and, having eliminated the numerous maintenance workers, he chose the drivers as models: imposing characters, equal to their task, they were the aristocracy of the carting business. Those hypervehicles were under their control for very considerable periods of time, not to mention the cargoes, which sometimes comprised all the goods and chattels of a magnate. Surely it would take a lifetime at least to travel in a straight line from Mendoza to Buenos Aires at a rate of two hundred meters per day. The cart drivers were transgenerational men; their gaze and manner were living records of the sublime patience exercised by their predecessors. Turning to more practical matters, it seemed that the key variables were weight (the cargo to be transported) and speed: the less the weight, the greater the speed and vice versa. Obviously the long-haul carters, given the flatness of the pampas, had opted to maximize weight.

And one day, suddenly, the carts set off ... A week later, they were still a stone's throw away, but sinking inexorably below the horizon. Rugendas, as he informed his friend, was possessed by an urgent, almost infantile desire to depart in their wake. He felt it would be like traveling in time: proceeding rapidly on horseback along the same route, they would catch up with carts that had set off in other geological eras, perhaps even before the inconceivable beginning of the universe (he was exaggerating), overtaking them all on their journey towards the truly unknown.

They set off on that trail. Following that line. A straight line leading all the way to Buenos Aires. What mattered to Rugendas, however, was not at the end of the line but at its impossible midpoint. Where something would, he thought, finally emerge to defy his pencil and force him to invent a new procedure.

The Godoys bid him farewell most affectionately. Would he come back one day? they asked. Not according to his itinerary: from Buenos Aires he would proceed to Tucumán, and from there he would head north to Bolivia and Peru, before eventually returning to Europe, after a voyage of several years ... But perhaps one day he would retrace his South American journey in reverse (a poetic idea that came to him on the spur of the moment): once again he would see all that he was seeing now, speak all the words he was speaking, encounter the smiling faces before him, identical, not a day younger or older ... His artist's imagination figured this second voyage as the other wing of a vast, mirrored butterfly.

They took an old guide, a boy to cook for them, five horses and two little mares (they had finally managed to get rid of the grumpy mules). The weather, still hot, became drier. In a week of unhurried progress, they left behind trees, rivers and birds, as well as the foothills of the Andes. A ruse against

Orphic disobedience: obliterate all that lies behind. There was no point turning around any more. On the plains, space became small and intimate, almost mental. To give their procedure time to adjust, they abstained from painting. Instead they engaged in almost abstract calculations of the distance covered. Every now and then they overtook a cart, and psychologically it was as if they had leapt months ahead.

They adapted to the new routine. A series of slight bumps indicated their way across the flat immensity. They began to hunt systematically. The guide entertained them with stories at night. He was a mine of information about the region's history. For some reason (no doubt because they were not practicing their art), Rugendas and Krause, in their daily conversations on horseback, hit upon a relation between painting and history. It was a subject they had discussed on many previous occasions. But now they felt they were on the point of tying up all the loose ends of their reasoning.

One thing they had agreed about was the usefulness of history for understanding how things were made. A natural or cultural scene, however detailed, gave no indication of how it had come into being, the order in which its components had appeared or the causal chains that had led to that particular configuration. And this was precisely why man surrounded himself with a plethora of stories: they satisfied the need to know how things had been made. Now, taking this as his starting point, Rugendas went one step further and arrived at a rather paradoxical conclusion. He suggested, hypothetically, that, were all the storytellers to fall silent, nothing would be lost, since the present generation, or those of the future, could experience the events of the past without needing to be told about them, simply by recombining or yielding to the available facts, although, in either case, such action could only be born of a deliberate resolution. And it was even possible that the repetition would be more authentic in the absence of stories. The purpose of storytelling could be better fulfilled by handing down, instead, a set of "tools," which would enable mankind to reinvent what had happened in the past, with the innocent spontaneity of action. Humanity's finest accomplishments, everything that deserved to happen again. And the tools would be stylistic. According to this theory, then, art was more useful than discourse.

A bird flashed across the empty sky. A cart immobile on the horizon, like a midday star. How could a plain like this be remade? Yet someone would, no doubt, attempt to repeat their journey, sooner or later. This thought made them feel they should be at once very careful and very daring: careful not to make a mistake that would render the repetition impossible; daring, so that the journey would be worth repeating, like an adventure.

It was a delicate balance, like their artistic procedure. Once again Rugendas regretted not having seen the Indians in action. Perhaps they should have waited a few more days ... He felt a vague, inexplicable nostalgia for what had not happened, and the lessons it might have taught him. Did that mean the Indians were part of the procedure? The repetition of their raids was a concentrated form of history.

Rugendas kept delaying the beginning of his task, until one day he discovered that he had more reasons for doing so than he had realized. A casual remark made beside the campfire provoked a rectification from the old guide: No, they were not yet in the renowned Argentinean pampas, although the country they were crossing was very similar. The real pampas began at San Luis. The guide thought they had simply misunderstood the word. And in a sense, they must have, the German reflected, but the thing itself was involved as well; it had to be. He questioned the guide carefully, testing his own linguistic resources. Were the "pampas," perhaps, flatter than the land they were crossing? He doubted it; what could be flatter than a horizontal plane? And yet the old guide assured him that it was so, with a satisfied smile rarely to be seen among the members of his grave company. Rugendas discussed this point at length with Krause later on, as they smoked their cigars under the starry sky. After all, he had no good reason to doubt the guide. If the pampas existed (and there was no good reason to doubt that either), they lay some distance ahead. After three weeks of assimilating a vast, featureless plain, to be told of a more radical flatness was a challenge to the imagination. It seemed, from what they could understand of the old hand's scornful phrases, that, for him, the current leg of the journey was rather "mountainous." For them, it was like a well-polished table, a calm lake, a sheet of earth stretched tight. But with a little mental effort, now that they had been alerted, they saw that it might not be so. How odd, and how interesting! Needless to say their arrival in San Luis, which was imminent according to the expert, became the object of eager anticipation. For the two days following the revelation they pressed on steadily. They started seeing hills everywhere, as if produced by a conjurer's trick: the ranges of El Monigote and Agua Hedionda. On the third day they came to expanses resonant with emptiness. The sinister nature of the surroundings made an impression on the Germans, and, to their surprise, on the Gauchos too. The old man and the boy talked in whispers, and the man dismounted on a number of occasions to feel the soil. They noticed that there was no grass, not the least blade, and the thistles had no leaves: they looked like coral. Clearly the region was drought stricken. The earth crumbled at a touch, yet a layer of dust did not seem to have formed, although they could not be sure, because the wind had dropped to nothing. In the mortal stillness of the air, the sounds of the horses' hooves, their own words and even their breathing were accompanied by menacing echoes. From time to time they noticed that the old guide was straining anxiously to hear something. It was contagious; they started listening too. They could hear nothing, except perhaps the faint hint of a buzzing that must have been mental. The guide clearly suspected something, but a vague fear prevented them from questioning him.

For a day and a half they advanced through that terrifying void. Not a bird to be seen in the sky, no guinea pigs or rheas or hares or ants on the ground. The planet's peeling crust seemed to be made of dried amber. When they finally came to a river where they could take on water, the guide's suspicions were confirmed. He solved the enigma, which was especially perplexing there on the river banks: not only were they devoid of the least living cell of vegetation, the numerous trees, mainly willows, had been stripped of all their leaves, as if a sudden winter had plucked them bare for a joke. It was an impressive spectacle: livid skeletons, as far as the eye could see, not even trembling. And it was not that their leaves had fallen, for the ground was pure silica.

Locusts. The biblical plague had passed that way. That was the solution, revealed to them at last by the guide. If he had delayed doing so, it was only because he wanted to be sure. He had recognized the signs by hearsay, never having seen them with his own eyes. He had also been told about the sight of the swarm in action, but preferred not to talk about that, because it sounded fanciful, though, considering the results, fancy could hardly have outstripped the facts. Alluding to his friend's disappointment at having missed the Indians, Krause asked if he did not regret having arrived too late on this occasion too. Rugendas imagined it. A green field, suddenly smothered by a buzzing cloud, and, a moment later, nothing. Could a painting capture that? No. An action painting, perhaps.

They proceeded on their way, wasting no time. It was idle to wonder which direction the swarm had taken, because the area affected was too large. They had to concentrate on getting to San Luis, and try to enjoy themselves in the meantime, if they could. It was all experience, even if they had missed out by minutes. The residual vibration in the atmosphere had an apocalyptic resonance.

As it turned out, a number of practical problems made it hard for the painters to enjoy themselves. That afternoon, after two days of involuntary fasting, the horses reached the limits of their endurance. They became uncontrollable, and there was no choice but to stop. To make things worse, the temperature had continued to rise, and must have been near one hundred and twenty two degrees. Not an atom of air was moving. The barometric pressure had plummeted. A heavy ceiling of grey clouds hung over their heads, but without affording any relief from the glare, which went on blinding them. What could they do? The young cook was frightened, and kept clear of the horses as if they would bite him. The old man would not raise his eyes, ashamed of his failure as a guide. There were attenuating circumstances: this was the first time he had crossed an area stricken by a plague of locusts. The Germans conferred in whispers. They were in a lunar ocean, rimmed around with hills. Krause was in favor of grinding up some biscuits, mixing them with water and milk, patiently feeding the horses with this paste, waiting a few hours for them to calm down and setting off again in the cool of the evening. For Rugendas, this plan was so absurd it did not even merit discussion. He proposed something a little more sensible: heading off at a gallop to see what was on the other side of the hills. Accustomed to reckoning distance in paintings, they misjudged the remoteness of those little mountains; in fact they were almost among them already. So the vegetation on their slopes had probably not been spared by the mobile feast. They consulted the guide, but could not get a word out of him. All the same, it was reasonable to suppose that the hills had served as a screen to deflect the swarm, so if they went around to the other side they would find a field with its full complement of clover leaves. Rugendas already had a plan: he would ride south to the hills, while his friend would ride north. Krause disagreed. Given the state of the horses, he thought it reckless to make a dash. Not to mention the storm that was brewing. He categorically refused. Tired of arguing, Rugendas set off on his own, announcing that he would be back in two hours. He spurred his horse to a gallop and it responded with an explosion of nervous energy; horse and rider were drenched with sweat, as if they had just emerged from the sea. The drops evaporated before they hit the ground, leaving a wake of salty vapor. The grey cones of the hills, on which Rugendas fixed his gaze, kept shifting as he rode on in a straight line; without becoming noticeably bigger, they multiplied and began to spread apart; one slipped around behind him surreptitiously. He was already inside the formation (why was it called El Monigote: The Puppet?). The ground was still bare and there was no indication that there would be grass ahead, or in any direction. The heat and the stillness of the air had intensified, if that was possible. He pulled up and looked around. He was in a vast amphitheater of interlayered clay and limestone. He could feel the horse's extreme nervousness; there was a tightness in his chest, and his perception was becoming abnormally acute. The air had turned a lead-grey color. He had never seen such light. It was a see-through darkness. The clouds had descended further still, and now he could hear the intimate rumbling of the thunder. "At least it will cool off," he said to himself, and those trivial words marked the end of a phase in his life; with them he formulated the last coherent thought of his youth.

What happened next bypassed his senses and went straight into his nervous system. In other words, it was over very quickly; it was pure action, a wild concatenation of events. The storm broke suddenly with a spectacular lightning bolt that traced a zigzag arc clear across the sky. It came so close that Rugendas's upturned face, frozen in an expression of idiotic stupor, was completely bathed in white light. He thought he could feel its sinister heat on his skin, and his pupils contracted to pinpoints. The thunder crashing down impossibly enveloped him in millions of vibrations. The horse began to turn beneath him. It was still turning when a lightning bolt struck him on the head. Like a nickel statue, man and beast were lit up with electricity. For one horrific moment, regrettably to be repeated, Rugendas witnessed the spectacle of his body shining. The horse's mane was standing on end, like the dorsal fin of a swordfish. From that moment on, like all victims of personalized catastrophes, he saw himself as if from outside, wondering, Why did it have to happen to me? The sensation of having electrified blood was horrible but very brief. Evidently the charge flowed out as fast as it had flowed into his body. Even so, it cannot have been good for his health.

The horse had fallen to its knees. The rider was kicking it like a madman, raising his legs till they were almost vertical, then closing them with a scissor-like clicking action. The charge was flowing out of the animal too, igniting a kind of phosphorescent golden tray all around it, with undulating edges. As soon as the discharge was complete, in a matter of seconds, the horse got to its feet and tried to walk. The full battery of thunder exploded overhead. In a midnight darkness, broad and fine blazes interlocked. Balls of white fire the size of rooms rolled down the hillsides, the lightning bolts serving as cues in a game of meteoric billiards. The horse was turning. Completely numb, Rugendas tugged at the reins haphazardly, until they slipped from his hands. The plain had become immense, with everywhere and nowhere to run, and so busy with electrical activity it was hard to get

one's bearings. With each lightning strike the ground vi-
brated like a bell. The horse began to walk with supernatural
prudence, lifting its hooves high, prancing slowly.

The second bolt of lightning struck him less than fifteen
seconds after the first. It was much more powerful and had a
more devastating effect. Horse and rider were thrown about
twenty meters, glowing and crackling like a cold bonfire.
The fall was not fatal, no doubt because of exceptional altera-
tions to atomic and molecular structure, which had the effect
of cushioning their impact. They bounced. Not only that,
the horse's magnetized coat held Rugendas in place as they
flew through the air. But once on the ground the attraction
diminished and the man found himself lying on the dry earth,
looking up at the sky. The tangle of lightning in the clouds
made and unmade nightmarish figures. Among them, for a
fraction of a second, he thought he saw a horrible face. The
Puppet! The sounds all around him were deafening: crash on
crash, thunderclap on thunderclap. The circumstances were
abnormal in the extreme. The horse was spinning around on
its side like a crab, cells of fire exploding around it in thousands, forming a sort of full-body halo, which moved with
the animal and did not seem to be affecting it. Did they cry
out, the man and his horse? The shock had probably struck
them dumb; in any case their cries would have been inau-
dible. The fallen horseman reached for the ground with his
hands, trying to prop himself up. But there was too much
static for him to touch anything. He was relieved to see the

horse getting up. Instinctively he knew this was a good thing: better the solitude of a temporary separation than the risk of a third lightning strike.

The horse did indeed rise to its feet, bristling and monumental, obscuring half the mesh of lightning, his giraffe-like legs contorted by wayward steps; he turned his head, hearing the call of madness . . . and took off . . .

But Rugendas went with him! He could not understand, nor did he want to—it was too monstrous. He could feel himself being pulled, stretching (the electricity had made him elastic), almost levitating, like a satellite in thrall to a dangerous star. The pace quickened, and off he went in tow, bouncing, bewildered . . .

What he did not realize was that his foot was caught in the stirrup, a classic riding accident, which still occurs now and then, even after so many repetitions. The generation of electricity ceased as suddenly as it had begun, which was a pity, because a well-aimed lightning bolt, stopping the creature in its flight, might have spared the painter no end of trouble. But the current withdrew into the clouds, the wind began to blow, rain fell ...

It was never known how far the horse galloped, nor did it really matter. Whatever the distance, short or long, the disaster had occurred. It was not until the morning of the following day that Krause and the old guide discovered them. The horse had found his clover, and was grazing sleepily, with a bloody bundle trailing from one stirrup. After a whole night spent looking for his friend, poor Krause, at his wits' end, had more or less given him up for dead. Finding him was not entirely a relief: there he was, at last, but prone and motionless. They hurried on and, as they approached, saw him move yet remain face down, as if kissing the earth; the flicker of hope this aroused was quenched when they realized that he was not moving himself, but being dragged by the horse's blithe little browsing steps. They dismounted, took his foot from the stirrup and turned him over ... The horror struck them dumb. Rugendas's face was a swollen, bloody mass; the bone of his forehead was exposed and strips of skin hung over his eyes. The distinctive aquiline form of his Augsburg nose was unrecognizable, and his lips, split and spread apart, revealed his teeth, all miraculously intact.

The first thing was to see if he was breathing. He was. This gave an edge of urgency to what followed. They put him on the horse's back and set off. The guide, who had recovered his guiding skills, remembered some ranches nearby and pointed the way. They arrived half way through the morning, bearing a gift that could not have been more disconcerting for the poor, isolated farmers who lived there. It was, at least, an opportunity to give Rugendas some simple treatment and take stock of the situation. They washed his face and tried to put it back together, manipulating the pieces with their fingertips; they applied witch hazel dressings to speed the healing and checked that there were no broken bones. His clothing was torn, but except for minor cuts and a few abrasions to his chest, elbow and knees, his body was intact; the major damage was limited to his head, as if it were the bearing he had rolled on. Was it the revenge of the Puppet? Who knows. The body is a strange thing, and when it is caught up in an accident involving nonhuman forces, there is no predicting the result.

He regained consciousness that afternoon, too soon for it to be in any way advantageous. He woke to pain such as he had never felt before, and against which he was defenseless. The first twenty-four hours were one long howl of pain. All the remedies they tried were useless, although there was not much they could try, apart from compresses and good will. Krause wrung his hands; like his friend, he neither slept nor ate. They had sent for the doctor from San Luis, who arrived the following night in the pouring rain on a horse flogged half to death. They spent the next day transporting the patient to the provincial capital, in a carriage sent by His Excellency the governor. The doctor's diagnosis was cautious. In his opinion the acute pain was caused by the exposure of a nerve ending, which would be encapsulated sooner or later. Then the patient would recover his powers of speech and be able to communicate, which would make the situation less distressing. The wounds would be stitched up at the hospital and the extent of the scarring would depend on the responsiveness of the tissue. The rest was in God's hands. He had brought morphine and administered a generous dose, so Rugendas fell asleep in the carriage and was spared the uncertainties of a night journey through quagmires. He woke in the hospital, just as they were stitching him up, and had to be given a double dose to keep him quiet.

A week went by. They took the stitches out and the healing proceeded rapidly. They were able to remove the bandages and the patient began to eat solids. Krause never left his side. The San Luis hospital was a ranch on the outskirts of the city, inhabited by half a dozen monsters, half man, half animal, the results of cumulative genetic accidents. There was no way to cure them. The hospital was their home. It was an unforgettable fortnight for Rugendas. The sensations impinging on the raw, pink flesh of his head were recorded indelibly. As soon as he could stand and go out for a walk on Krause's arm, he refused to go back in. The governor, who had surrounded the great artist with attentions, offered his hospitality. Two days later Rugendas began to ride again and write letters (the first was to his sister in Augsburg, presenting his misfortunes in an almost idyllic light; by contrast, the picture he painted for his friends in Chile was resolutely grim). They decided to leave without delay. But not to follow their original route: the unknown immensity separating them from Buenos Aires was a challenge they would have to postpone. They would return to Santiago, the nearest place where Rugendas could receive proper medical treatment.

For his recovery, though miraculous, was far from complete. He had hoisted himself out of the deep pit of death with the vigor of a titan, but the ascent had taken its toll.

Leaving aside the state of his face for the moment, the exposed nerve, which had caused the unbearable suffering of the first days, had been encapsulated, but although this meant the end of the acute phase, the nerve ending had reconnected, more or less at random, to a node in the frontal lobe, from which it emitted prodigious migraines. They came on suddenly, several times a day; everything went flat, then began to fold like a screen. The sensation grew and grew, overpowering him; he began to cry out in pain and often fell over. There was a high-pitched squealing in his ears. He would never have imagined that his nervous system could produce so much pain; it was a revelation of what his body could do. He had to take massive doses of morphine and the attacks left him fragile, as if perched on stilts, his hands and feet very far away. Little by little he began to reconstruct the accident, and was able to tell Krause about it. The horse had survived, and was still useful; in fact, it was the one he usually chose to ride. He renamed it Flash. Sitting on its back he thought he could feel the ebbing rush of the universal plasma. Far from holding a grudge against the horse, he had grown fond of it. They were fellow survivors of electricity. As the analgesic took effect, he resumed his drawing: he did not have to learn again, for he had lost none of his skill. It was another proof of art's indifference; his life might have been broken in two, but painting was still the "bridge of dreams." He was not like his ancestor, who had to start over with his left hand. If only he had been so lucky!

What bilateral symmetry could he resort to, when the nerve was pricking at the very center of his being?

He would not have survived without the drug. It took him some time to metabolize it. He told Krause about the hallucinations it had caused during the first few days. As clearly as he was seeing his friend now, he had seen demonic animals all around him, sleeping and eating and relieving themselves (and even conversing in grunts and bleats!) . . . Krause undeceived him: that part was real. Those monsters were the poor wretches interned for life in the San Luis hospital. Rugendas was stunned by this, until the onset of the next migraine. What an amazing coincidence! Or correspondence: it suggested that all nightmares, even the most absurd, were somehow connected with reality. He had another memory to recount, different in nature, although related. When they took the stitches out of his face, he was vividly aware of each thread coming loose. And in his addled, semiconscious state, he felt as if they were removing all the threads that had controlled the puppets of his feelings, or the expressions that manifested them, which came to the same thing. Averting his gaze, Krause made no comment and hastened to change the subject. Which was not so easy: changing the subject is one of the most difficult arts to master, the key to almost all the others. And in this case, change was a key part of the subject.

For Rugendas's face had been seriously damaged. A large scar descended from the middle of his forehead to a piglet's nose, with one nostril higher than the other, and a net of red streaks spread all the way to his ears. His mouth had contracted to a rosebud puckered with furrows and folds. His chin had been shifted to the right, and transformed into one big dimple, like a soupspoon. This devastation seemed to be irreversible, for the most part. Krause shuddered to think how fragile a face was. One blow and it was broken forever, like a porcelain vase. A character was more robust. A psychological disposition seemed eternal by comparison.

Even so, he might have grown accustomed to that mask, talking to it, waiting for replies, even predicting them. But the worst thing was that the muscles, as Rugendas himself had intuited in his fantasy about the threads, no longer responded to his commands; each one moved autonomously. And they moved much more than normal. It must have been because of the damage to the nervous system. By chance, or perhaps by miracle, this damage was limited to Rugendas's face, but the contrast with his calm trunk and limbs made it all the more striking. The twitching would begin with a slight quiver, a trembling, then spread suddenly and within seconds his whole face was jerking in an uncontrollable St. Vitus's dance. It also changed color, or colors, becoming iridescent, full of violets, pinks and ochres, shifting constantly as in a kaleidoscope.

Viewed from that protean rubber, the world must have looked different, thought Krause. Hallucinations colored not only Rugendas's recent memories but also the scenes of his daily life. On this subject, however, he remained discreet;

he must have been still getting used to the symptoms. And no doubt he did not have time to follow a line of thought through to its conclusion, because of the attacks, which occurred once every three hours, on average. When the pain came on, he was possessed, swept away by an inner wind. He hardly needed to explain what was happening: it was all too visible, although he did say that in the grip of an attack he felt amorphous.

A curious verbal coincidence: amorphous, morphine. The drug went on accumulating in his brain. With its help he began to practice his art again, and organized his routine around spells of pain relief and drawing. In this way he recovered a certain degree of normality. The physiognomic procedure sustained his undiminished skill. The charmingly intimate landscapes of San Luis provided ideal subjects for his convalescent exercises. Nature, in its nineteen vegetal phases, adapted itself to his perception, enveloped with Edenic light: a morphine landscape.

An artist always learns something from the practice of his art, even in the most constraining circumstances, and in this case Rugendas discovered an aspect of the physiognomic procedure that had so far escaped his notice. Namely that it was based on repetition: fragments were reproduced identically, barely changing their location in the picture. If this was not immediately obvious, not even to the artist, it was because the size of the fragments varied enormously, from a single point to a panoramic view (which could greatly exceed the dimensions of the picture). In addition, the fragment's outline could be affected by perspective. As small and as large as the Taoist dragon.

Like so many discoveries, this one seemed at first to be purely gratuitous. But perhaps one day it would have a practical application.

After all, art was his secret. He had conquered it, although at an exorbitant price. He had paid with everything else in his life, so why not the accident and the subsequent transformation? In the game of repetitions and permutations, he could conceal himself even in his new state, and function unseen like any other avatar of the artist. Repetitions: in other words, the history of art.

Why this obsession with being the best? Why did he have to assume that only quality could legitimize his work? In fact, he could hardly even begin to think about it except in terms of quality. But what if he was making a mistake? Or indulging in an unhealthy fantasy? Why couldn't he be like everyone else (like Krause, for example), simply painting as well as he could and giving more weight to other things? That kind of modesty could have considerable effects; for a start it would allow him to practice other arts, should he wish . . . or all of them. His medium could become life itself. The absolutist ambition came from Humboldt, who had designed the procedure as a universal knowledge machine. But that pedantic automaton could be dismantled without giving up the array of styles, each of which was a kind of action.

Within ten days they were back in Mendoza (a journey of one hundred and fifty miles): they rode the same horses along the same route and passed the same carts, accompanied by the same guide and the same cook. The only thing that had changed was Rugendas's face. And the direction. They were slightly delayed by the rain, the wind and the way things looked the same. The Godoy family, notified of the ghastly incident weeks before, renewed their hospitality, but this time they tactfully provided a separate room, where the painter would have more peace and quiet, while still enjoying all the benefits of being in the family's care. His room was perched on the roof; it had once been a lookout, before the trees around the house blocked the view. They could offer him the use of it now because the heat was easing off (it was mid-March); in midsummer, it was a kiln.

Solitude was good for him: he was beginning to cope on his own, and it was a relief to do without Krause for a whole day at a time—not that he was in any way annoyed by the presence of his faithful friend, who was an ideal companion, but because he wanted to leave him in peace, to let him go out and amuse himself in Mendoza after his bedside vigils. He abhorred the thought of being a burden. Secluded in his dovecote, he began to regain his self-esteem, in so far as it was possible.

Those were days of introspection and soul-searching. He had to assimilate what had happened and try to find a viable way forward. He played out internal debates in his correspondence, to which he devoted a great deal of time. He filled pages and pages with his small, compact handwriting. Throughout his life he was a prolific letter writer: clear, organized, explicit, precise. Nothing escaped him. As his letters have been preserved, there is no shortage of documentary material for his biographers, and although none of them has tried, it would be perfectly possible to reconstruct his travels day by day, almost hour by hour, following every movement of his spirit, every reaction, every scruple. The treasure trove of his letters reveals a life without secrets, yet somehow still mysterious.

There were two reasons for his feverish activity during those first days in Mendoza. He was behind in his correspondence, since all he had sent from San Luis were a few brief, faltering notes in a shaky hand, containing a bare minimum of information and making promises to elaborate later, which it was now time to fulfill. But he also needed to clarify things for himself and come to terms with the gravity of his situation, and the only means of doing so at his disposal was the familiar practice of letter writing. That is why there is so much information directly or indirectly related to this episode, concerning not only the events themselves but also their intimate repercussions. The artist's mastery of documentation had carried over to the rest of his life, becoming second nature to the man.

His first and principal correspondent was his sister Luise, back in his hometown of Augsburg. With her he was touchingly sincere. He had never hidden anything from her and could not see why he should do so now. Yet at this juncture he discovered that Luise could not take in the whole range of possible documentation. Or, rather: although she could (because there were no secrets between them), certain things would be left out. This was one of those situations in which the whole is not enough. Perhaps because there were other "wholes," or because the "whole" made up by the speaker and his personal world rotates like a planet, and the combined effect of rotation and orbital movement is to keep certain sides of certain planets permanently hidden. To use a modern term, which does not appear in the letters, we might call this a problem of "discursive form." As if he had been aware of it from the start, Rugendas had prudently built up a range of correspondents scattered around the globe. So now he resumed the task of writing to other addresses; among his interlocutors he counted physiognomic painters and naturalists, ranchers, farmers, journalists, housewives, rich collectors, ascetics and even national heroes. Each set the tone for a different version, but all the versions were his. The variations revolved around a curious impossibility: how could he communicate the proposition "I am a monster"? It was easy enough to set it down on paper. But transmitting its significance was far more difficult. In the case of his Chilean friends the problem was pressing, and he took particular care over his letters to them, especially the Guttikers, who had already written inviting him to stay at their house in Santiago, as he had before setting out on his journey a few months before. Since they would be seeing him shortly, he felt he had to warn them. The obvious thing to do in this case would have been to exaggerate, in order to diminish the surprise. But it was not easy to exaggerate, given the state of his face. He ran the risk of falling short, especially if they were allowing for obvious exaggeration. Which would make the surprise even worse.

In any case, he certainly did not shut himself away. His body's natural regimen required a good deal of fresh air and exercise. And even in his semi-invalid state, in spite of the frequent migraines, the nervous attacks and the constant medication, it became imperative for him to dedicate the hours of good daylight to riding and painting the natural world. The faithful Krause never left his side, because the attacks could occur far from the house, in which case he would hoist Rugendas onto his own horse and gallop back, undaunted by the cries of pain. Those spectacular crises were not, however, the most remarkable aspect of their outings. Rugendas attracted a great deal of attention even when he was behaving with perfect calm and propriety. People gathered to look at him, and in half-civilized places like the picturesque environs of Mendoza, one could hardly expect discretion to be the rule. The children were not the worst, because the adults behaved like children too. They watched him intently drawing the large hydraulic devices used for irrigation (his latest enthusiasm), and they were consumed by the desire to see his papers. What did they imagine? As for Rugendas, each time he took up his pencil he had to resist the temptation to sketch himself.

At summer's end the weather had attained ultimate perfection. The landscapes took on an infinite plasticity; the shifting light of the Cordillera enveloped them hour by hour, made them transparent, endless cascades of detail. The afternoon light, filtered by the imposing stone ramparts of the Andes, was a ghost of its morning self, an optics of the mind, inhabited by the untimely pinks of midafternoon. Twilight went on for ten or twelve hours. And during the friends' night walks, gusts of wind rearranged stars and mountains. If it was true, as the Buddhists said, that everything, even a stone, a dead leaf or a blowfly, had already existed and would exist again, that everything was part of a great cycle of rebirths, then everything was a man, a single man on the scale of time. Any man, Buddha or a beggar, a god or a slave. Given sufficient time, all the elements of the universe would combine to form a man. This had major consequences for the procedure: for a start, it could not operate automatically like a transcendent mechanics, with each fragment being slotted into its predetermined place; each fragment could become any other, and the transformation would be accomplished not in the dimension of time but in that of meaning. This idea could give rise to a totally different conception of reality. In his work, Rugendas had come to the conclusion that the lines of a drawing should not represent corresponding lines in visible reality, in a one-to-one equivalence. On the contrary, the line's function was constructive. That was why the practice of drawing remained irreducible to thought, and why, although he had completely incorporated the procedure, he could continue to draw.

The Godoys had still not grown accustomed to his new appearance. This was an interesting sign of things to come. People can get used to any deformity, even the most frightful, but when it is accompanied by an uncontrollable movement of the features, a fluid, senseless movement, habit has no stable base on which to build. Perception remains correspondingly fluid. Although sociable and talkative by nature, Rugendas began to retire shortly after dinner and spend the evenings on his own. This he could do without awkwardness, since he had a legitimate excuse: struck down by superhuman migraines, he was at first incapable of anything but writhing on the bed of his attic room ... and not only the bed, on the floor too, and the walls, and the ceiling ... when the medication took effect, he returned to his letters.

In his writing he tried to be absolutely sincere. He reasoned as follows: in principle, telling the truth and lying require the same amount of effort, so why not tell the truth, without omissions or ambiguities? If only as an experiment. But this was easier to say than to do, especially since in this case the doing was a kind of saying.

Perhaps the morphine would never be metabolized. Perhaps he was entering a second or a third phase. Or was the combination of the opiate, the migraines and the nervous meltdown of a physiognomic landscape painter producing an unprecedented result? In any case the concept of truth took on monstrous proportions in his imagination, and rent his nights in the little rooftop room.

The letters from this period are much concerned with an apparently extraneous matter, to which Rugendas returns obsessively, like a monomaniac. His book *A Picturesque Voyage through Brazil*, the basis of his considerable fame throughout Europe, had in fact been written by someone else, the French journalist and art critic Victor Aimé Huber (1800–1869), using Rugendas's manuscript notes. Although this had not struck him as irregular at the time, it now seemed very odd indeed, and he wondered how he could have consented to such a scheme. Surely it was fraudulent to publish a book under the signature of X when it had in fact been written by Y? He had been so distracted by the whole process of the publication, which was absurdly complicated because of the nature of the book, that he had agreed without thinking. There were so many tasks involved, from financing the project to the coloring of the plates; the writing of the text seemed a mere detail. The lithographs were the book's main attraction: a hundred of them, executed by French artists, except for three, which Rugendas had done himself. Although the lithographers, Engelmann & Co., had a well-deserved reputation as the finest in Europe, he still had to supervise the preparation of the lithographs in person and in minute detail; the process consisted of various stages and was beset with pitfalls. He had thought of the text as an accompaniment to the images; but what he had not seen at the time, and was now beginning to realize, was that by considering it an accompaniment or a complement he was separating the text from the "graphic" content. And the truth, he now saw, was that both were part of the same thing. Which meant that the ghostwriter, the "nègre," had infiltrated the very essence of the work, under the pretext of carrying out a purely technical task: making coherent sentences out of the disjointed scraps of oral documentation. But everything was documentation! That was where it all began and where it ended too. Where it began especially (because the end was far off down the misty ways of science and art history). Nature itself, preformed by the procedure, was already documentation. There were no pure, isolated data. An order was implicit in the phenomenal revelation of the world; the order of discourse shaped things themselves. And since his current mental state was part of that order, he would have to examine it and find rational explanations for what seemed to be a visionary or maniacal chaos. It should be added here that Rugendas was not medicating himself with pure morphine—which could not be synthesized at the time—but with a tincture of opium in a bromide solution. This combined the benefits of the best analgesic and those of the best antidepressant. His face twitched like a second hand timing an eternity of Buddhist reincarnations. It was one way to cure the "publishing pains" resulting from his past errors of judgment.

Although in their letters the Guttikers kept urging him to return to Chile, the journey across the mountains was repeatedly postponed. He was engrossed in the work of letter writing and still apprehensive about confronting acquaintances with his new face, while the need for medical attention had become less urgent, partly because his torments had settled into a more or less stable pattern and partly because he was beginning to accept the futility of any treatment. But the preponderant reason for the delay was that conditions in Mendoza at that time of year were ideal for painting. And this, in turn, encouraged the two friends to extend their excursions, in so far as Rugendas's health permitted, always venturing southwards, towards the forests and lakes, where, despite the cold, a mysterious tropical zone of blue light and endless foliage seemed to begin. They would spend the night in San Rafael, a little village ten leagues south of the provincial capital, or at one of the ranches in the area belonging to friends or relatives of the Godoys, and then set off, sometimes for whole days at a time, up winding valleys, in search of views, which they captured in increasingly strange watercolors. After a few such exquisite outings, they could not bear to give them up. The vagueness of the letters Rugendas wrote during those weeks has allowed a legend to spring up, according to which he journeyed far into the south, to regions unexplored by white men, perhaps all the way to the fabled glaciers, shifting mountains of ice, impregnable portals of another world. The field sketches dating from that time lend credence to the myth. They have an air of impossible distance about them. For the legend to be true, Rugendas would have had to fly through the air, like an Immortal, from the known to the unknown. Which is what he was doing all the time, mentally. But for him it was a normal, everyday activity, a mere background for incredible events, anecdotes or episodes.

Whatever the truth of the matter, the Germans found themselves in natural surroundings that were excitingly unfamiliar, so unfamiliar that Rugendas required confirmation from his friend that what he was seeing existed objectively and was not a product of his altered state. Urgent, impertinent birds flung outlandish cries in the tangled vegetation, guinea fowl and hairy rats scampered away before them, powerful yellow pumas kept watch from rock ledges. And the condor soared pensively over the abysses. There were abysses within abysses and trees rose like towers from the deep underground levels. They saw gaudy flowers open, large and small, some with paws, others with rounded kidneys of apple flesh. In the streams there were siren-like molluscs and, at the bottom, always swimming against the current, legions of pink salmon the size of lambs. The deep green of the araucaria trees thickened to a velvety black or parted to reveal floating landscapes that always seemed upside down. Around the lakes, forests of delicate myrtle, with trunks like tubes of yellow rubber, smooth to the touch and cold as ice. Moss plumped up to form wilderness sofas;

the airy lacework of fern fronds quivered nervously.

And then one day they remembered: when the Indians mounted their deadly, lightning raids, it was from those zones that they emerged. It would not have surprised them to learn that they appeared from thin air. But obviously they came from a place on earth, somewhere further away, who knows where, and the forests flanking the Cordillera provided them with handy passages for making quick incursions into civilization and equally quick getaways. They were reminded of these events, which had greatly exercised Rugendas's imagination before the accident, not by an association of ideas, but by reality itself, in the most abrupt manner. They had spent the night at a ranch near San Rafael, after three days of camping at high altitude amid Edenic greenery. During the descent they had decided to go straight back to Mendoza, but then they stopped to paint and had to spend the night at the ranch house, whose owner was coming to the end of his summer stay on the property and preparing to return to town, where his children went to school. Rugendas, who was going through a particularly critical phase, had attacks of vertigo and cerebral short-circuiting all night; he could only withstand them by taking an excessive dose of morphine, and dawn found him sleepwalking, covered in sweat, his face a jig of lightning tics, his pupils shrunk to pinpoints as if he were at the center of the sun.

And when the sun rose the yard began to resound with shouts and the noise of horses.

Indians! Indians!

What?

Indians! Indians!

The household swung into action in an instant; it sounded as if all its occupants were hurling themselves against the walls like raving lunatics. The two friends came to the door of their room, which opened onto a gallery around the yard. Krause intended to find out what was happening, how serious the disturbance was and if there was any possibility of setting out for Mendoza, while his friend went back to bed; but Rugendas came out after him, half-dressed and staggering. Krause could have stood on his authority and sent him back, but it was not worth the trouble: in the confusion, no one would pay any attention to the monster's somnolent bumbling, and besides there was no time to lose. So he let him reel freely.

The men were organizing the defense. It was not the first time they had taken up arms to drive the Indians back, nor would it be the last, and their manner was relaxed. It was simply part of the job. But the customary nature of the occurrence had not led to improved organization; how could the response be organized when the raids were so erratic and unpredictable? With a bare minimum of information they improvised a counterattack, as swift as possible, and combined, as best they could, with an emergency roundup, because the main aim was to limit the losses of livestock.

According to a messenger, the attack had begun at dawn with a massacre at the post office, and spread from there as the Indians went rustling cattle all around the area. They could not have advanced much further and mounted parties were already setting out in pursuit from the surrounding ranches. The number of Indians was estimated at one thousand; it was a medium-to-large raid.

A contingent of farmhands would remain at the ranch house to defend the women and children; the house, as the owner told Krause, could be transformed into a fort using simple panels, which were already being put into place. He asked what the Germans were intending to do; they could be useful either way, going along or staying behind.

This conversation, interrupted by shouts and orders (and energetic gestures), took place in the middle of the yard, where the men were already gathering with their guns. Krause, still half asleep, was of two minds, and went back to see if his friend had returned to the room . . . but no, there he was, using a hat to cover his face, still as a tree. He gave a violent start when Krause took him by the arm. Asked if he had heard the news, he mumbled indistinctly in reply . . . No, he had clearly neither heard nor understood what was happening. Krause decided immediately to put him back to bed and stay to help with the defense of the house, if it came to that. He could not help feeling a twinge of regret: they had cherished the dream of seeing the Indians in action, and now their chance had come, but they would have to miss it. While the ranch owner and his men made a noisy exit through the gates, Krause took his friend's arm and started leading him back to the house. To stop him falling in the other direction, he had to guide him from behind, gripping both arms and holding him up. Rugendas walked stiffly but all the parts of his body seemed to be working loose. He went on mumbling, and since Krause was ignoring him, raised his voice to a shout. They were already back in the gallery. Krause came around to face him, and, rather embarrassed, asked what he was saying. It was something about a mantilla. Krause opened the door of the room and Rugendas darted in, went straight to his painting kit, and pointed to his friend's. Krause could not believe his eyes, but he had to bow to the evidence: in spite of the state he was in, the great Rugendas wanted to go and sketch the Indian raid. Krause sat down on the bed disconsolately. It's impossible, impossible, he said. Rugendas paid no attention. He had realized he was barefoot and begun the laborious business of putting on his boots. He looked up at Krause: The horses, he said. Krause tried a dissuasive argument that had just occurred to him: they could sleep for a couple of hours and leave around midday. The action was bound to continue into the afternoon. But Rugendas was not listening; he was in another dimension. His movements had transformed the room into a mad scientist's laboratory where some transformation of the world was being hatched. The nocturnal half-light gave the interior a Flemish touch. Like a purple-faced lion he fumbled with his boots, on all fours. Krause rushed out, heading for the stables, pursued by the stammering of his half-shod friend: Man! Manti! Mantilla! They would take only Flash and the bay horse, Dash. It would not have to be more than an outing, after all, a painter's picnic; and perhaps the ride and the activity would help to clear Rugendas's mind. He had probably overexerted himself during the previous days, because of the abundance of beauty they had encountered. The raid had come at a bad time, and yet it could still serve a purpose: to exhaust the painter's energy, or rather, to complete that process; given his current state the only hope of improvement lay in plumbing the depths.

Rugendas was waiting for him in the yard with his little box of charcoal sticks and his hat pulled down over his face. He kept talking about a mantilla, and Krause finally understood what he meant. It was a good idea; he should have thought of it himself, but he could hardly be blamed, what with everything else he had to think of. I'll go and see, he said, and tell our hostess what we are planning to do. Rugendas went with him, and when they found the lady of the house, in the kitchen, it was the invalid who summoned all his ebbing strength to make the unusual request for a lace mantilla, of the kind worn at mass, black, naturally, it went without saying. South American ladies were well supplied with such Catholic accessories. He did not explain in detail why he needed it, and she must have supposed it was to hide the hideous disfigurement of his face and his ghastly nervous tics. In which case, she can only have been surprised that he had taken so long to equip himself with that charitable disguise. For inhabitants of Mendoza (as for Chileans), the idea of a man wearing a mantilla was not so strange, because there was a long and venerable tradition of "masked men" in the region. In any case, it was a situation in which people kept making peremptory demands for the most incongruous objects without a word of explanation. She sent someone to fetch the mantilla, and while they were waiting, gave them some indication of where the fighting was taking place and how the sides were maneuvering. The idea of going out to paint the action struck her as splendid; she was sure they would capture some interesting images. But they had to remember to take precautions, and not get too close. Were they armed? Both had revolvers. No, there was no need to worry about her; the house was safe. It was not the first time she had been through this exercise and it no longer scared her. They even exchanged jokes; the hardy pioneers made light of the absurdity of the age. Their scale of values accommodated the most outrageous nuisances. For them, the Indians were simply part of reality. So the foreigner wanted to paint them? They could see nothing strange in that.

The mantilla arrived; it was made of fine black lace. Rugendas took it reverently, and the first thing he did was to gauge its transparence, which was, it seemed, to his satisfaction. He took his leave without further ado, promising to return the mantilla intact that evening. By then, said the lady with a heroic laugh, I may be Madame Pehuenche. God forbid! exclaimed Krause, bowing to kiss her outstretched hand.

So they set off. A farmhand held the yard gate open; it would be barred behind them. Rugendas was waving the mantilla like a madman, and he bumped into one of the pillars of the gallery. Up they leapt onto their horses. But Rugendas landed facing backwards, looking at the tail. The animals took off; he covered his face with the mantilla, put his hat on top of it, and knotted it around his neck ... But when he came to look for the reins of course he could not find them. The horse was headless! That was when he realized he was sitting backwards, and turning around was a nightmare circus trick. By the time he had pulled it off (Krause, embarrassed, had gone ahead), they were already out of the yard, and the enormous grilles shut behind them with a *clang* to which the birds replied.

The beautiful San Rafael morning greeted them with songs of freedom. The sun was rising behind the trees. They rode side by side. Rested and docile, Flash and Dash stepped evenly, their faces inexpressive. Is everything all right? asked Krause. Yes! Are you all right? Yes! And it was true: he looked absolutely fine, with the mantilla covering his face. It hid the damage. Although, of course, that was not why he had chosen to wear it. He had wanted something to filter the light. Direct sunlight tormented his poor addled head and his shattered nervous system. His pinpoint pupils could not contract any further; the drug had deactivated the adaptive reflex and even moderate illumination soon became too much for him. It was as if he had taken another step into the world of his paintings. By virtue of a curious phenomenon of conditioning, Krause kept guessing at the absurd grimaces hidden by the black lace.

The morning was truly glorious, perfect for a raid. There was not a cloud in the sky; the air had a lyrical resonance; birds were combing the trees. The lid had been taken off the world specifically to reveal the conflict, the clash of civilizations, as at the dawn of history. They came to a vast prairie, heard shots in the distance and set off at a gallop.

Krause did not write letters, or if he did, no one bothered to keep them. So his thoughts can only be reconstructed in an indirect or speculative manner. Rugendas remarked repeatedly that he seemed to be preoccupied (describing his own state in the letters, he tended to use Krause as a rhetorical device, a supplementary "color": the feelings attributed to his friend, or, in some instances, invented for him, served to express what tact or shame prevented Rugendas from saying about himself, for example, "K. thinks that the quality of my sketches has not declined"). While continuing to fulfill his self-imposed duties, if anything with greater vigilance, Krause withdrew into a melancholy abstraction. As they rode out that day he was assailed by gloomy thoughts about the state of his friend's health. He felt guilty about going along with his mad plan, and not just because it was mad: agreeing to it was like saying "What the hell," like granting a dying man his last wish. All his reactions were colored by the idea that death had come between them and struck a blow, whether fatal or a mere foretaste was immaterial for the moment. In the course of a journey one encounters so many people, such a mass of humanity, that to be singled out seemed unjust. Yet since it was so natural not to ask of another "Why him?," the question "Why me?" seemed scandalous and impossible. Of course in Krause's case it was not "Why me?" but "Why him?" Nevertheless the close bond between the two men gave the question a new twist, producing its most disturbing form: "Why not me?" This made Krause think of himself as a survivor, an inheritor, a vessel for his friend's whole life, dragged along by an immense force of time. If, as he had often felt, simplifying intuitively, he and Rugendas made up all of humanity, each of them was equally likely to be struck down. And whichever it was, the balance would be maintained. After all, this splendid raiding day might be remembered as "the day Krause died." That was why they stayed together, in spite of everything that could have driven them apart. Having a partner was a way of outliving oneself, in life and in death. And although, regrettably, this led to feelings of guilt and nostalgia, the resulting melancholy had a role to play in the general system of euphoria: only melancholy generated good ideas about the dead, and those ideas could contribute to the procedure.

Indian fever was catching. Where where they? Rugendas and Krause rode off into the radiant dawn in search of them, as in an illustration. By chance they came across a path, which must have led to the post office, so they followed it at a dash, hearing shots closer and closer at hand, then shouts. It was the first time they had heard Indians.

They passed through a series of parallel windbreaks and the action came into view, the first action of that memorable day. In the distance, the white post office, tiny like a die. Closer, a party of ranchers on horseback, shooting into the air, and the Indians, on horseback too, galloping around and shouting. Everything was moving very quickly, including them, as they rushed down into the little valley at full tilt. The engagement, like all the others they were to witness, operated as follows: the savages were equipped only with cutting and stabbing weapons, pikes, lances and knives; the white men had shotguns, but they used them to fire warning shots into the air, thus keeping the enemy far enough away to render their weapons ineffective. And so they skirmished back and forth. This balance could only be maintained at high velocity: both sides kept accelerating, and as the other side had to keep up, they reached their physical limits almost immediately. The scene was very fluid, very distant, a mere optical play of appearances ...

They could not let this pass; they had to draw it. And they did, without dismounting, resting the paper on portable drawing boards. When they looked up again, there was no one left. Krause glanced across at his friend's sketch. It was strange and disturbing to see him sketching with his head hidden in that black cocoon. He asked if Rugendas could see properly.

He had never seen better in his life. In the depths of that mantled night the pinpricks of his pupils woke him to the bright day's panorama. And powdered poppy extract, a concentrated form of the analgesic, provided sleep enough for ten reawakenings per second.

They put their papers into the saddlebags and spurred the horses on, for this scene had been a mere appetizer. And as they came out of the valley (beginner's luck!) they saw a hundred or so Indians veering off to the north, no doubt heading for one of the undefended ranches in the area. This provided subjects for more sketching; Rugendas filled five sheets before the group disappeared from view. As they were setting off again, they encountered a band of ranchers, whom they were able to inform of the Indians' movements. They could be useful, even while keeping out of the mêlée.

On their own again, they headed southwards at walking pace, exchanging their first impressions. Luckily both of them had good eyesight. It seemed they would have to resign themselves to seeing the Indians in miniature, like lead soldiers. Yet the details were all there, violently impressed on their retinas, magnified on the paper. In fact, if they wanted to, they could draw isolated details. The detail that fascinated them was the brevity of it all, the way organization emerged from chance, the speed of the organization. The procedure of the combat between Indians and white men mirrored that of the painters: it was a matter of exploiting the balance between proximity and distance.

Coming over a rise they saw more action: this time the Indians were beating a hasty retreat up a rocky slope, the horses scrambling like goats, leaving behind dozens of rustled bull calves, while the ranchers fired through the gaps in the herd. The scene was picturesque in the extreme. The stick of charcoal began to fly across the paper. The mountain, lit by perpendicular sunlight, offered the racing figures a fan of escape routes, like a peacock's open tail. The artists had to be careful not to exaggerate in their depiction, for the Indian horsemen in their ascent could easily become so many variations on Pegasus. Yet realism was guaranteed as long as they kept sketching naturally, and in that sense having to draw quickly and work out the perspective as they went was a help.

When the Indians had disappeared, they galloped over to the ranchers to see what they were doing. The shots had taken their toll on the herd. Some of the bull calves had been killed; others were still standing, stunned. The men were arguing about brands, which were all mixed up, and nonexistent on some of the recently weaned animals. The Germans were surprised to discover that brands could be objects of dispute; they had always thought of them as signs designed to be read unequivocally. They learnt that troops from the fort were engaged in hand-to-hand combat in the stockyards at El Tambo, two leagues away. Thanking the ranchers for this information, they set off.

But halfway there they had to stop again, for the fourth

time, to sketch a scrap at a stream crossing. They were starting to feel that there were Indians everywhere. As is often
the case with collectors, the problem was not a lack but an
excess of specimens. The devils were obviously using disper-
sion as an added weapon.

It was like wandering from room to room at a party, from
the living room to the dining room, from the bedroom to
the library, from the laundry to the balcony, all full of noisy,
happy, more or less drunk guests, looking for a place to cud-
dle or trying to find the host to ask him for more beer. Except
that it was a house without doors or windows or walls, made
of air and distance and echoes, of colors and landforms.

This stream could have been the bathroom. The Indians
wanted to charge but they were retreating; the white men
wanted to retreat, but in order to do so they had to charge (in
order to scare the enemy more effectively with their bangs).
This ambivalence was driving the horses crazy; they plunged
into the water, splashed about, or simply stopped to drink,
very calmly, while their riders yelled themselves hoarse in
simultaneous flight and pursuit. The skirmish had an infinite
(or at least algebraic) plasticity, and since Rugendas was ob-
serving it at closer range this time, his flying pencil traced details of tense and lax muscles, wet hair clinging to supremely
expressive shoulders. . . Everything sketched in this explosive
present was material for future compositions, but although
it was all provisional, a constraint came into play. It was as if
each volume captured in two dimensions on the paper would

have to be joined up with the others, in the calm of the studio, edge to edge, like a puzzle, without leaving any gaps. And that was indeed how it would be, for the magic of drawing turns everything into a volume, even air. Except that for Rugendas the "calm of the studio" was a thing of the past; now there was only torment, drugs and hallucinations.

The savages scattered in all directions, and four or five came climbing up the knoll where the painters had stationed themselves. Krause drew his revolver and fired twice into the air; Rugendas was so absorbed that his only reaction was to write BANG BANG on his sheet of paper. The sight of his head wrapped in black lace must have frightened the Indians, for they veered away immediately and made off across the hillside. The painters went down to the stream, where their horses drank. They had come a long way, and what with one thing and another, the morning was already half gone. They struck up a conversation with the men who had remained by the crossing. They were soldiers from the fort; they had ridden from El Tambo in pursuit of the Indians, and were about to return. They could go all together.

Krause was intrigued by the fact that neither these men nor those they had met earlier seemed in the least taken aback by the mask covering Rugendas's face. Yet their lack of surprise was logical enough, since in such difficult situations, adapting any object to any purpose was the norm. In everyday life there were explanations for everything, and in abnormal circumstances, there were explanations for the explanations.

Apparently there was a regular battle underway at El Tambo; the soldiers wanted to leave immediately. Krause suggested that he and Rugendas rest for an hour or so on the shady banks of the stream; he was worried about his friend's state of overexcitement and the effect it might have on his system. But Rugendas would not listen: he had not even begun; there was so much to do, right now! And from his point of view, he was right: he had not begun, and he never would.

Off they went, with the young soldiers, who joked and bragged about their comical exploits. It all seemed fairly innocuous. So this was an Indian raid? This series of tableaux vivants? There was still a possibility that it could live up to the popular image, turning ugly and barbaric. But if not, what did it matter?

They did not reach El Tambo. Halfway there, Rugendas had an attack, a severe one. The soldiers were alarmed by his cries and the way he writhed on the saddle. Krause had to tell them to continue on their way, he would take care of it. There was a little hill close by and as the artists struck out in that direction, Rugendas pulled off his hat and flung it away, punching at his temples. What had really shaken the soldiers was not being able to see the origin of the cries, hidden inside the black mantilla. They could not link them to a subjective expression. Oddly, it was the same for Krause. After hours of riding and drawing together without seeing his friend's face, the cries made him realize that he could no longer reconstruct its appearance.

They dismounted in the shade. Between convulsions, Rugendas took all his remedies at once, without measuring the doses, and fell asleep. He woke up half an hour later, free of acute pain but in a delirious daze. The only thread attaching him to reality was an urgent desire to follow the events at close hand. By this stage, of course, the raid seemed to be simply one more hallucination. He was still wearing the mantilla, and must have needed it more than ever now. Krause did not dare ask him to remove it for a moment so he could see his face. He was beginning to speculate wildly about what might be hidden behind the lace. He tried to stop thinking about it, but could not help himself. Lifting Rugendas back into the saddle, he was amazed by the coldness of his body.

In terms of the physiognomy of combat, the best was still to come, at El Tambo. They sketched the battle from various points of view, for hours, until after midday. It was an uninterrupted parade of Indians, compensating for the brevity of their appearances by repeating them. Rugendas found himself making pluralist sketches. But wasn't that what he always did? Even when he drew one of the nineteen types of vegetation identified by the procedure, he was taking its reproduction into account, seeing it as part of a multitudinous species, which would go on making nature. Continually reappearing from the wings, the Indians were, in their way, making history.

The postures they adopted on horseback were beyond belief. This exhibitionism was part of a system for inspiring fear at a distance. There was something circus-like about it, with shooting instead of applause. They didn't care about the laws of gravity, or even whether the full value of their performance was being appreciated; the postures, it is true, had no value in themselves. Rugendas would have to rectify them on paper, to make them plausible in the context of a static composition. But in his sketches the rectification was incomplete, so traces of their real strangeness remained, archeological traces in a sense, because they were overlaid and obscured by speed.

Mounted squads emerged periodically from El Tambo—a complex of low buildings adjoined by extensive corrals— with all their firearms blazing, momentarily breaking the rings of savages, which reformed within seconds. The dairy cows had lain down; they looked like dark lumps. The dances of the Indian horsemen attained extremes of fantasy when it came to displaying their captives. This was a distinctive feature of the raids, almost a defining trait. Stealing women, as well as livestock, was what made it all worthwhile. In fact, it was an extremely rare occurrence, and functioned more as excuse and propitiatory myth. Unsuccessful as usual, the Indians at El Tambo displayed the captives they had not been able to take, with defiant and, again, extremely graphic gestures.

They came around the hill by the stream, a little group of them, lances raised, yelling: Huinca! Kill! Arrghh! The loudest, in the middle of the group, was triumphantly holding a "captive," perched sideways on the neck of his horse. Naturally this was not a captive at all, but another Indian, disguised as a woman; he was making effeminate gestures, but no one could have fallen for such a crude trick, and even the Indians seemed to be treating it as a joke.

Whether for fun or to make a symbolic point, they took it further. An Indian rode past comically cuddling a "captive" which was in fact a white calf. The soldiers intensified their fire, as if the taunts had enraged them, but perhaps that was not the reason. The next display took extravagance to the limit: the "captive" was an enormous salmon, pink and still wet from the river, slung across the horse's neck, clasped by a muscular Indian, who was shouting and laughing as if to say: "I'm taking this one for reproduction."

All these scenes were much more like pictures than reality. In pictures, the scenes can be thought out, invented, which means that they can surpass themselves in terms of strangeness, incoherence and madness. In reality, by contrast, they simply happen, without preliminary invention. There at El Tambo, they were happening, and yet it was as if they were inventing themselves, as if they were flowing from the udders of the black cows.

Had the artists been close to the action, it would have been impossible to transfer it to paper, even using some kind of shorthand. But distance made a picture of it all, by including everything: the Indians, the path by the stream, El Tambo, the soldiers, the cart track, the shots, the cries and the broader view of the valley, the mountains and the sky. They had to shrink everything down to a dot, and be ready to reduce it further still.

Within each circle there was a transitive, transparent cascade, from which the picture recomposed itself, as art. Tiny figures running around the landscape, in the sun. Of course, in the picture, they could be seen close up, although they were no bigger than grains of sand; the viewer could come as near as he liked, subject them to a microscopic scrutiny. And that would bring out the hidden strangeness: what would be called "surrealism" a hundred years later but was known, at the time, as "the physiognomy of nature"; in other words, the procedure.

The parade continued, at varying speeds. It seemed the riders would never tire. Suddenly all the soldiers came out at once and the Indians scattered, heading for the mountains. Taking advantage of the informal truce that ensued, our friends entered El Tambo, where a wake was being held. One of the dairy farmers had been killed by the Indians early that morning. The women had put his body back together. So there had been one casualty at least. The two Germans respectfully asked permission to draw the corpse. They reflected that it would not be easy to find the culprit, were anyone to try. Then they visited the labyrinthine stock-yards and accepted an invitation to lunch. There was roast meat and nothing else, not even bread. "Roast Indian," said the soldier turning the spit, with a guffaw. But it was veal, very tender and cooked to perfection. They drank water, because there was a busy afternoon ahead. Since everyone else was retiring for the siesta, Krause was able to persuade Rugendas to rest for a while. They went and lay down on the banks of the stream.

Krause was intrigued. He had not expected his friend to bear up under the strain, yet he seemed willing to keep going, although not to show his face. He had eaten very little, barely lifting the hem of his lace mask away from his chin, and when his friend had diffidently asked if it was not awkward to eat like that, he had replied that the midday light would wound his eyes like a knife. It was the first time Krause had seen him so cautious, even on days of very bright light and after having ingested large quantities of analgesics. No doubt the circumstances were exceptional. Still it was odd for someone so fastidious to persist in wearing a grease-spattered mantilla.

Rugendas took some more powdered poppy extract, but remained awake behind the opaque black lace. As Krause was not sleepy either, they looked over their drawings and discussed them. There was certainly no shortage of material, but they were not so sure about its quality and the subsequent reconstruction. Both of them had been making these discrete sketches with the sole aim of composing stories, or scenes from stories. The scenes would be part of the larger story of the raid, which in turn was a very minor episode in the ongoing clash of civilizations. There is an analogy that, although far from perfect, may shed some light on this process of reconstruction. Imagine a brilliant police detective summarizing his investigations for the husband of the victim, the widower. Thanks to his subtle deductions he has been able to "reconstruct" how the murder was committed; he does not know the identity of the murderer, but he has managed to work out everything else with an almost magical precision, as if he had seen it happen. And his interlocutor, the widower, who is, in fact, the murderer, has to admit that the detective is a genius, because it really did happen exactly as he says; yet at the same time, although of course he actually saw it happen and is the only living eyewitness as well as the culprit, he cannot match what happened with what the policeman is telling him, not because there are errors, large or small, in the account, or details out of place, but because the match is inconceivable, there is such an abyss between one story and the other, or between a story and the lack of a story, between the lived experience and the reconstruction (even when the reconstruction has been executed to perfection) that widower simply cannot see a relation between them; which leads him to conclude that he is innocent, that he did not kill his wife.

Something else the Germans had to take into account, as they remarked in their conversation, was that the Indian was an Indian through and through, right down to minimal fragments, such as a toe, from which the whole Indian could be reconstructed, although they had a different example in mind: not a toe or a cell, but the pencil stroke on paper tracing the outline of a toe or a cell.

All this led Krause to a conclusion that was almost as bewildering as the story of the innocent assassin: compensation was alien to the Indians. In fact this conclusion derived from a thought that had often crossed his mind (and not only his): every physical defect, however minor or inevitable, even the gradual, imperceptible wear and tear of aging, requires a compensation, in the form of intelligence, wisdom, talent, practical or social skills, power, money, etc. This was why Krause the dandy attached so much importance to his physical appearance, his elegance and his youth: they allowed him to dispense with everything else. And yet, as a civilized man, he could not escape from the compensatory system. Painting, his art of choice, was a way of complying with its minimal requirements. Requirements which, until that day, he had considered absolute; without a minimum of compensation it would be impossible to go on living. But that was before he had seen the Indians, and now he had to admit that they did not respect the minimum—on the contrary, as objects of painting, they made fun of it. The Indians had no need of compensation, and they could allow themselves to be perfectly coarse and unpleasant without feeling any obligation to be well dressed and elegant to make up for it. What a revelation it was for him!

But no sooner had he said this than he remembered the state of his poor friend's face (hidden though it was behind the mantilla) and began to worry about how Rugendas might interpret his disquisition.

Needless scruples, for his friend was plunged in the deepest of hallucinations: the non-interpretive kind. In a sense, Rugendas was the one who had taken non-compensation to the limit. But he did not know this, nor did it matter to him.

The proof of this achievement was that while conversing silently with his own altered state (of appearance and mind), he continued to see things and, whatever those things were, they seemed to be endowed with "being." He was like a drunk at the bar of a squalid dive, fixing his gaze on a peeling wall, an empty bottle, the edge of a window frame, and seeing each object or detail emerge from the nothingness into which it had been plunged by his inner calm. Who cares *what* they are? asks the aesthete in a flight of paradox. What matters is *that* they are.

Some might say these altered states are not representative of the true self. So what? The thing was to make the most of them! At that moment, he was happy. Any drunk, to pursue the comparison, can vouch for that. But, for some reason, in order to be happier still (or unhappier still, which comes to the same thing, more or less) one has to do certain things that can only be done in a sober state. Such as making money (which more than any other activity requires a clear head) so as to go on purchasing elation. This is contradictory, paradoxical, intriguing, and may prove that the logic of compensation is not as straightforward as it seems.

Reality itself can reach a "non-compensatory" stage. Here it should be recalled that Mendoza is not in the tropics,

not even by a stretch of the imagination. And Humboldt
had developed his procedure in places like Maiquetía and
Macuto ... in the midst of that peculiarly tropical sadness:
night falling suddenly, without twilight, the sea washing
back over Macuto again and again, futile and monotonous,
the children always diving from the same rock ... And what
for? What were they living for? So they could grow up to
become ignorant primitives and, worse, deplorable human
ruins by the time they reached maturity.

In the afternoon everything became stranger still. The
action had shifted away from El Tambo, so the two Germans
set off in search of more views, guided by noises and hearsay.
If the San Rafael valley was a crystal palace, and the tributary
valleys its wings and courtyards, the Indians were coming
out of the closets, like poorly kept secrets. The scenes followed one another in a certain order, but their traces on
paper suggested other orders, which, in turn, affected the
original scenes. As for the landscape, it remained indifferent.
The catastrophe simply came in on one side and went out
on the other, changing nothing in between.

The Germans continued with their work. New impressions of the raid replaced the old ones. Over the course of
the day, there was a progression—though it remained incomplete—towards unmediated knowledge. It is important
to remember that their point of departure was a particularly
laborious kind of mediation. Humboldt's procedure was, in
fact, a system of mediations: physiognomic representation

came between the artist and nature. Direct perception was eliminated by definition. And yet, at some point, the mediation had to give way, not so much by breaking down as by building up to the point where it became a world of its own, in whose signs it was possible to apprehend the world itself, in its primal nakedness. This is something that happens in everyday life, after all. When we strike up a conversation, we are often trying to work out what our interlocutor is thinking. And it seems impossible to ascertain those thoughts except by a long series of inferences. What could be more closed off and mediated than someone else's mental activity? And yet this activity is expressed in language, words resounding in the air, simply waiting to be heard. We come up against the words, and before we know it, we are already emerging on the other side, grappling with the thought of another mind. *Mutatis mutandis*, the same thing happens with a painter and the visible world. It was happening to Rugendas. ⌐What the world was saying was the world.⌐

And now, as if to provide an objective complement, the world had suddenly given birth to the Indians. The noncompensatory mediators. Reality was becoming immediate, like a novel. The only thing missing was the notion of a consciousness aware not only of itself but of everything in the universe. Yet nothing was missing, for the paroxysm had begun.

The afternoon was not a repetition of the morning, not even in reverse. Repetition is always a matter of waiting, rather than the repeated event itself. But in the grip of the paroxysm, there was no waiting for anything. Things simply happened, and the afternoon turned out to be different from the morning, with its own adventures, discoveries and creations.

In the end, Rugendas collapsed, slumping onto the paper, struck down by a terrible cerebral seizure. Faint moans could be heard emerging from the balloon of black lace, inflated and deflated by his labored breathing. He slipped over Flash's neck, his stick of charcoal still pirouetting in the air, and fell to the ground. Krause got down to help him. Off in the distance, against a superb background of pinks and greens, the Indians were scattering, so tiny they could have been mounted on mosquitoes.

Like a Mater Dolorosa, Krause held the unconscious body of his friend and master, under crowns of foliage multiplied to infinity. The trills of a sky-blue cephalonica encircled the silence. Night was falling. It had been falling for some time.

In the last, miraculously drawn-out light, soldiers and ranchers gathered at the fort to debrief. The horses were exhausted. The riders hung their heads, speaking in mournful grunts; all were grimy, their faced powdered with dust, some were falling asleep in the saddle. Krause joined one of the parties, with Rugendas slung over the back of his horse, sleeping off a dose of powdered poppy extract, his head hanging level with the stirrup, which gave it a ding like a bell's clapper at every step. The mantilla, however, had remained in place. Night had fallen by the time they reached the fort, and they reached it none too soon, for the darkness was absolute.

Rugendas woke at two, in a dreadful state. Swinging back and forth between sickness and health throughout the course of that incredible day had left him a wreck. Yet he resumed his work without a moment's delay. And the strangest thing was that he did not remove his mantilla, simply because he had forgotten that he was wearing it. He and Krause were in the situation room at the fort, feebly lit by a pair of candles; a murky gloom reigned in that vast space. The poor painter could see nothing through the veil, but did not realize. His vision had been so perturbed during the day, that not being able to see made no difference to him now. Thrashing about blindly, he was an outlandish sight, and his shuffling of the papers attracted the other men's attention. He had taken it into his head to classify the scenes, and since he could not see them, he got so mixed up that the contortions of his body, understandably limited by his shattered nerves, seemed to be mimicking the postures of the Indians. Krause could not bear to see him make a spectacle of himself and slipped out discreetly, as if he were going to relieve himself. Less tactful, the soldiers and ranchers gazed in wonder at the puppet with the wrapped-up head. The obvious solution would have been to tear the rag off, but this did not occur to Rugendas because he was so used to it, while, for precisely the opposite reason, the others were too stunned to act; there was only one person who, being in between these extremes, might have done the sensible thing, but he was not present.

At that moment, Krause was experiencing a revelation of his own. Depressed and preoccupied, he had gone out into the blackest of nights. He could sense the forests and mountains as pure afterimages, black forms plunged in an ocean of black. After an uncertain lapse of time spent in melancholy rumination, he suddenly realized he could see everything: the mountains, the trees, the paths, the panoramas with their slightly dreamy perspectives ... Was he seeing or remembering? He marveled at the faculty of sight, its prodigious, ultra-physiognomic capacities, the dilation of the pupil, the brain's interpretations. In fact, the moon had come out, that was all. And yet he had not been mistaken.

Back inside, the men had been waiting for the moonlight so they could return to their respective homes. They put on their hats and went out. That was when Rugendas, who had not been entirely oblivious to their conversations, noticed the owner of the ranch where he had stayed the previous night, and by association, remembered his wife and what she had lent him, at which point he finally raised his hands to his face, felt the lace, realized he was still wearing the mantilla and pulled it off without bothering to untie the knots. In spite of the fact that it was now a filthy, malodorous rag, soiled with grease, sweat and dust, he held it out, trying to make his numb tongue articulate words of thanks intended for the rancher's wife. All eyes were fixed on him, in wonder as much as in fright. When the rancher was finally able to respond, he mumbled a no, still mesmerized by Rugendas. What he meant to say was that the painter could return the mantilla himself and thank his wife in person, since he would presumably be returning to the ranch with them to spend the night. But when the monster insisted, he took the rag, and as there was nothing more to say, let the conversation lapse and stood there staring. What an ugly sight! The reason he had initially refused the filthy shroud was that, unconsciously, he had wanted to say: Keep it on.

They all came out together, and when Krause saw them, he went to fetch the horses; he too was assuming that they would return to the ranch from which they had set out that morning. As he approached the group, leading the two beasts, it took him a moment to realize that Rugendas had removed his mask. He had grown used to it too, from the other side. His friend's face, fully illuminated by the moonlight, seemed larger now and more frightful. He froze for a moment. The men were beginning to mount and ride off. Krause had thought they would have to carry Rugendas, but there he was, standing, steady enough, except for his face. His face occupied the compartments of the night. Was the moon illuminating his face or was it the other way around?

Be that as it may, Rugendas had made other plans. To Krause's astonishment, he had plans for the rest of the night. Incredible as it seemed, he wanted to go on working. What did it matter if he was ill, since the remedies he had taken allowed him to begin again with undiminished energy? And what could be more common than the act of beginning again? It was being repeated all the time. What else could really be repeated? In the beginning was Repetition, and only there. It was Krause, not Rugendas, who by virtue of his health, was moving along an unbroken line, a continuum, without beginning or end.

Krause did not understand what Rugendas had said to him. The painter's face overpowered everything else, even speech. Besides, there was no time to talk, since they were already riding, just the two of them, not towards the ranch but into the forest, drawn into the twisting funnels and bottlenecks, the horses clattering like bronze octopuses, southwards, towards the unknown, guided by the painter's facial compass. Tall, slender silhouettes, as if they were riding giraffes, all in black yet visible, they sped on, sucked towards another and a further slice of space, slipping in among the black's grey shades. The sound of the galloping hooves preceded them and bounced back, warning of obstacles. In that sense they were like bats. Like the bats that abound in those mountains and come streaming out of their caves at that time of night. And they could feel them brushing past! It is extremely uncommon to feel the touch of a bat, because those little creatures are equipped with infallible anti-crash devices. But a touch is not a crash, and occasionally sheer speed makes a touch unavoidable. Which is what happened to Rugendas on this occasion. A bat coming in the opposite direction brushed gently against his forehead. The contact lasted barely a hundredth of a second; it was hardly distinguishable from a breeze or the chance stimulation of a cell. But in the world of nature, there is always an explanation for delicacy. And this delicacy was supreme, incomparable, not only because of the mechanism that produced the contact, but also because of the material that sensed it: a forehead in which all the nerves had been torn loose. What could possibly be gentler or subtler?

This last part of the episode is even more inexplicable than the rest. Yet we cannot doubt that the events really took place, since the artist recorded them in his subsequent correspondence. In his letters he apologizes to family and friends, and principally to his sister, for what he calls his "daring"—though "recklessness" might have been more apt—in going to observe the Indians at close quarters, so he could complete the day's sketches, filling in the foregrounds. There is, of course, a certain irony in his words. After all, what could have happened? They might have killed him. A minor detail. In any case, by the time his correspondents saw the resulting pictures, that is by the time his work reached European galleries or museums, he would certainly be dead. The artist, as artist, could always be already dead. There was something absurd about trying to preserve his life. An accident, big or small, could kill a man, or a thousand, or a thousand million men at once. If night were lethal, we would all die shortly after sunset. Rugendas might have thought, as people often do: "I have lived long enough," especially after what had happened to him. Since art is eternal, nothing is lost.

He was in the lead. He had heard the soldiers at the fort say that, after a battle, the Indians usually camped close by. Weary of the distances that had given form to the raid, they could not wait to have done with them and stopped a stone's throw away.

For that reason, or perhaps because the Germans had been riding so quickly, they arrived almost at once. Beside a waterfall, on a broad platform of pink schist, the Indians were dining. They had built fires and were sitting in circles around them. Not a thousand of them. That had been an exaggeration. A hundred. The stolen cattle were in a small field nearby, surrounded by the horses to stop them from wandering. The Indians had butchered twenty for ribs and sirloins to roast, and had already begun to eat. To say that they were astonished to see the monstrous painter break into the circle of light would be an understatement. They did not believe their eyes. They could not. It was an all-male gathering: no women or children were present. Had they wanted to, whatever they might have said, the Indians could have taken the plunder back to their tents, a few hours' ride away. But they had decided to make a night of it: using the raid as an excuse, they had left their women waiting, worried and famished. Not that they needed to get away from the women to get drunk and go wild; they were capping off the foray with a binge, just to please themselves and to hell with the others. The drinking had begun with an aperitif, in the local manner. They swigged from the bottles they had managed to steal. Drunkenness and guilt fused into terror when they saw that moonlit face, that man who had become all face. They did not even notice what he was doing: all they could see was him. They would never have been able to guess why he was there. How could they know that there was such a thing as a procedure for the physiognomic representation of nature, a market hungry for exotic engravings, and so on? They did not even know that there was an art of painting, and although they possessed that art in some different, equivalent form, they could not establish the equivalence.

So Rugendas was able to enter the circle of firelight undisturbed, open his pad of good canson paper and go to work with charcoal and red chalk. Now he really was at close range and every detail was visible: big mouths with lips like squashed sausages, Chinese eyes, figure-eight noses, locks matted with grease, bull necks. He drew them in the blink of an eye. The paradoxical effect of the morphine had made him extra quick in his application of the procedure. He went from one face to another, one sheet to the next, like a lightning bolt striking a field. And the resulting psychic activity ... A brief aside is apposite here: psychic activity is normally translated into facial expressions. In the case of Rugendas, whose facial nerves had been lacerated, the "representation commands" from the brain did not reach their destination; or rather they did, unfortunately, but scrambled by dozens of synaptic confusions. His face expressed things he did not mean to express, but no one realized, not even Rugendas, because he could not see himself. He could only see the faces of the Indians, which to him were horrible too, but all in the same way. His face was not like any other. It was like the things that no one ever sees, like the reproductive organs viewed from inside. Not exactly as they are—in that case they would be recognizable—but badly drawn.

The tongues of flame flickered higher, splashing the Indians with golden light, illuminating a detail here, another there, or plunging everything into a sudden wave of darkness, animating the absent gesture, endowing mindless stupor with a continuous activity. They had begun to eat, because they couldn't resist, but everything they did led them back to the center of the fable, where drunkenness was mounting. Following their foray, a painter had emerged from the night to reveal the delirious truth of the day's events. Owls began to moan deep in the woods and the terrified Indians were captured in swirls of blood and optical effects. In the dancing firelight, their features drifted free. And although they were gradually beginning to relax and crack rowdy jokes, their gazes kept converging on Rugendas: the heart, the face. He was the focal point of that waking nightmare, the realization of the terrifying possibility that had haunted the raid in its various manifestations over the years: physical contact, face to face. As for the painter, he was so absorbed in his work that he remained oblivious to the rest. In the depths of that savage night, intoxicated by drawing and opium, he was establishing contact as if it were simply another reflex. The procedure went on operating through him. Standing behind him, hidden in the shadows, the faithful Krause kept watch.

24th of November, 1995